CW00500159

MAX'S CAMPERVAN CASE FILES BOOK 2

SLAUGHTER AT THE Seaside

TYLER RHODES

Copyright © 2023 Tyler Rhodes

All rights reserved. This book or any portion thereof may not be reproduced or used in any manner whatsoever without the express written permission of the author except for the use of brief quotations in a book review.

This is a work of fiction. Names, characters, businesses, places, events and incidents are either the products of the author's imagination or used in a fictitious manner. Any resemblance to actual persons, living or dead, or actual events is purely coincidental.

Dedicated to everyone who's ever thought, *"I bet it will clear up,"* then regretted going camping.

Chapter 1

"Anxious, stop being rude!" I warned my over-excited Jack Russell Terrier as he skidded to a halt next to a family of four and began drooling over their limp sandwiches.

Usually never a nuisance to other people, and always well-behaved, Anxious kept his eyes glued to the picnic the mother and father were trying to hand out to two giggling daughters even more excited than Anxious to be at the beach.

I hurried across the baking sand, hissed the naughty dog's name yet again, and he deigned to turn to look at me with the saddest puppy dog eyes you could ever imagine.

"Can we give him a sandwich, Daddy?" asked the younger girl as her mother tried to rub sunscreen into her sand-encrusted body, much to her protestations.

"No, honey, you must never feed other people's animals. The owner might not like it."

"But he's so hungry," the elder child whined as she scooted away from her sunscreen-wielding father who'd decided the lunch could wait until I'd got Anxious under control.

"He always looks like that when there's food around," I said, smiling apologetically as I approached. "He's had his breakfast, and we've been playing for over an hour already, but he knows that if he looks mournful he can get a treat. Don't let him fool you though."

"Will he bite us, mister?" asked the smaller girl, eyes wide.

"Anxious only bites bad people. Are you bad?"

Frowning, the girl put a finger to her cheek, deep in thought, then admitted, "I once had three biscuits when Daddy said I could only have one."

"That's just a misdemeanour, not a serious crime, so I think you're safe."

She nodded, seemingly satisfied, then asked, "Can I stroke him?"

"Sure, as long as your parents say it's okay. Be gentle, but don't feed him as nobody wants a fat Jack Russell lazing about the place."

Both girls made a fuss of Anxious, who was only too happy to oblige. He loved people, he loved food, and he loved to play. Add in chasing rabbits and the book was written for my constant companion of several years. Best friend, shoulder to cry on, ear to bend while I recounted my woes, Anxious and I were a team, and a good one.

Fuss over, I called for him to leave the family and this time he did as I asked. We continued our stroll along Abergele Beach after we had a few words about him pestering people.

With poo bags in my pocket, ball flinger in my hand, and Anxious darting in and out of the water to retrieve his ball, I felt like the luckiest man in the world.

The sun was shining on a perfect Thursday in June, with the whole long summer ahead of me. The forecast was for months of warm, dry weather, with next to zero chance of rain during an unprecedented heatwave. We hadn't reached those heady heights yet, but with the temperature into the mid-to-high twenties it was comfortable, the sky was an achingly beautiful blue, and the water was clear, still, and dazzling. Another day in paradise for us after a rocky start to our new vanlife adventure.

Campervans, cooking, and corpses summed up our first few days of vanlife, with the bodies piling up along with the steep learning curve living in a VW 1967 T1 split screen campervan, but for all the upset and inconvenience I wouldn't have changed a thing.

We had everything we needed, minus one ex-wife, and life was good.

Now staying further west along the North Wales coastline at a cute campsite that was beyond back-to-basics, consisting of a field, a toilet and shower block, and absolutely nothing else, including people, we'd decided to remain in the area for the week to settle in properly to our new way of life and allow me the chance to get Vee, my campervan, properly organised now I'd fallen into a routine.

There was so much to adjust to, so many things to remember, and so many previously inconsequential matters to consider that I'd never given a second thought before, but there was no denying that I, and Anxious, were loving it. This way of life needed some serious compromise, but the rewards were worth it. I felt connected to the world around me in a way I never had. At one with the country and its people, closer to nature and, incongruously, like I lived in a massive house rather than a rusty old metal box on ancient wheels. The outdoors was little more than a step away at any given moment, and I adored it.

With my long brown hair—now streaked with grey —and the beard growing nicely, for the first time in many years it felt like I was back to being me. How I should have always looked, and always behaved. Max Effort, man who had put his life as a Michelin 3-star restaurant chef behind him and truly become the person he was destined to be.

Free.

Whistling, I smiled at people walking along the long, sandy stretch of beach that'd been raked smooth and clear of any debris, presumably by a machine early that morning to make it perfect for the tourists. I waved at children playing with buckets and spades, laughed at fathers being buried in the sand by eager children, and stopped to watch with a little jealousy as people roared across the water on jet-skis. I wondered what that would be like, but figured Anxious would be less than keen, and knew I wasn't about to risk an injury as the life of a nomad meant I had to ensure I remained fit and able.

Anxious raced back from the water and dropped his orange ball at my feet, so I picked it up using the flinger and watched as it sailed into the shallows. The energetic pooch was off like a shot, never tiring of this most excellent of games. He bounded in, splashing chaotically, then swam out a little ways, grabbed the ball, and hurried back to repeat the process all over again.

We replayed the game as we made our way along the beach towards the busiest area where more families congregated and dogs weren't allowed to be off the lead. The safe zone meant it was a no-go for us, as who wants to hear a Jack Russell whine? But we had to pass through as the other side of this zone was where the shallows afforded excellent rock pools and we could search for crabs, another favourite pastime of ours. Anxious never tired of chasing after them, and getting pincered on the nose meant he now had a lifelong foe to growl at. His eyes lit up as I told him about the rock pools, so I clipped him on the lead and we hurried past the swarm of holidaymakers, weaved around the small lifeguard station on raised stilts where a bored-looking man who must have been younger than Anxious sat scanning the water in the hopes of rescuing a beautiful, tanned, bikini-clad damsel in distress to alleviate the monotony.

Once in the dog-friendly section, I unclipped Anxious and he raced ahead, barking about his freedom to anyone who would listen and everyone who wouldn't, then halted abruptly, kicking up sand, where someone's children had done a wonderful job of burying their parent.

I breezed past, smiling at the mound of sand far along the beach away from the densely populated area. The foot sticking out of the sand was very red, and the poor guy would pay for that tonight when the sunburn really kicked in. How long had he been there for?

Anxious barked once more, so I threw the ball for him but he stayed put, which wasn't like him.

I stopped and turned, something not feeling quite right, then it registered. Where was the rest of him? I hadn't seen his head in the sand. That wasn't normal. We needed our heads. They were one of the most important bits. Especially the breathing holes.

Anxious was digging furiously with his front paws, throwing sand behind him in a frenzy as he whimpered in consternation. Dashing back over, I stood to the side and watched as my small white dog with cute brown patches worked studiously. The mound of sand was just as you'd expect when someone was buried by their children, but as I'd thought, there was just the shape of a body, with no visible head grinning at me.

And wouldn't the person be shouting at Anxious? And where were the kids?

"Okay, I think that's enough, buddy," I said, knowing something wasn't right here but nothing really registering properly.

Anxious whined, and with one final big burst of activity he went loco in the sand. I bent and grabbed his collar to calm him down and caught the unmistakable smell of slowly cooking meat. Or was it rot? The foot was bright red and the skin was blistering, but the underlying colour was wrong, almost like it was... What was it? Bloodless? Was that what my mind was trying to assimilate? A foot without blood. Shrunken, and just plain wrong.

The hole that Anxious had dug around the protruding foot began to fill with sand as it slid from around the ankle, revealing a ragged stump.

The foot toppled sideways, startling us both. I released Anxious, and he ran circles around me as I scooted back and sat in the baking sand, staring at the severed foot slowly roasting on this otherwise perfect June day.

I glanced around, but there was nobody near us, just people sunbathing or families enjoying themselves if they had children young enough to not be in school. Several people walked past along the shoreline, talking happily, everyone enjoying themselves.

But I felt cold, and I felt beyond weird.

Why on earth was there a foot buried in the sand to make it look like there was a person here? Knowing I had to be sure, I inched forward on hands and knees and scooped the sand away from the outline, dreading what I might find, but also what I might not.

"Please don't let there be a severed head, or an arm, or any gross inside bits," I muttered as the dry sand slid through my fingers, rough and warm.

There was nothing, so I moved back and wondered what I should do. Scream for help? Run off and get someone? Call the police? I shouldn't leave this appendage unattended. What if a dog took it, or a child found it?

And then I laughed. Realisation hitting me. This was a joke, right? Someone was playing a game. I looked around again, expecting to find a group of sniggering teens pointing and laughing, but nobody was paying us any attention whatsoever. I waited. Maybe they were biding their time until I stood, screaming, and ran away.

Nobody came, so I turned my attention back to what I was now suspecting wasn't a fake foot at all. It had sunburn, and was smelly, and rubber feet didn't do that. Not that I had any experience of rubber feet, mind you.

"Anxious, listen to me," I told him, voice low and serious.

He sat and cocked his head, attention focused.

"I need to go and get help. Sit and guard. Sit and guard. Anxious, stay."

He wagged happily, always keen to show off how much he understood and how clever he was, so I backed away keeping an eye on him, then turned and hurried towards the lifeguard station.

The tanned young man, slim and muscular and clad only in a pair of crimson shorts, was leaning against the rail of the raised platform, binoculars focused on the shore. I called up and he lowered them then slowly turned his head, his mop of curly blond hair bouncing in the sunlight, a glassy look in his eyes as though he was having trouble staying awake.

"I found a foot," I mumbled. The words sounded dumb, but what was I supposed to say?

"Huh?" said the kid with a frown as he brushed a curl behind his ear.

"I said, I found a foot in the sand. Over there, where my dog is."

"What kind of foot?" he asked as he came down the steps, his shorts clinging to muscular thighs.

"A severed one. Of a man, I think. Although, I guess it could be a woman's. It was buried, sticking out like someone had got their kids to play."

"So some dude is enjoying time with his kids," shrugged the bored lifeguard.

"No, he isn't, because there is no rest of him. Just the foot. You better come take a look. Can you call the police?"

"Mate, I'm not calling anyone," snapped the man, scowling. "I hate jokes like this. Why do you people think it's okay to mess us around? This is a serious job and people rely on me. I can't be bothered with your nonsense."

He turned and began to go up the steps to resume his duties, but I put my hand to his elbow and said, "I'm not messing about. Why would I? Come and see."

"You better not be fooling around," he muttered, then descended again. "Show me where. But seriously, dude, a foot? That's lame. And not funny."

"You'll see," I grunted, feeling sorry for the kid because he probably got sent on all kinds of fake emergencies by bored children winding him up.

I led him over to Anxious where he remained guarding his find. Luckily, nobody seemed to have come this way, so everything was how it had been.

I pointed at the foot, and said, "See?" trying not to blanch at the sight of the flies.

"Very good," the lifeguard laughed, stepping forward. "It looks real. Okay, fun's over, but yeah, you got me. You can get up now," he said to the body-shaped mound. Obviously, nothing happened, so he marched forward and nudged the sand with his foot, causing it to collapse and reveal nothing but more of the same. He spun to me, eyebrows raised, and asked, "You aren't kidding, are you?"

"No, it's real. Look, it's even sunburned."

Fair play to the youngster, although he was most likely early twenties, he scooted over and bent then turned to me and said, "Must have been here hours for it to be so red."

"When was high tide?"

"Very early morning. About four. This stretch was clear by at least five, and it won't be back in for hours. That's so gross." He stood and asked, "You see anyone? Where was the foot?"

"I didn't see anyone, and it was just sticking up as though someone was lying down."

"Why would someone do that? Why bother with the pretence?"

"No idea," I shrugged. "I'm Max by the way. And that's Anxious."

Anxious barked happily, then came over and rubbed against the lad's bare leg.

"Trevor, but everyone calls me Trev. I can't believe it's a foot. How cool is this?"

"Cool?"

"Um, you know, in a gross way, but this job's so boring. Nobody ever nearly drowns, and nothing ever happens. But this is awesome!" he beamed, rubbing his hands together.

"Tell that to Mr. No Foot."

"Well, yeah, obviously it's awful and alarming and all that jazz, but it's exciting, too, right?"

"Trust me, discovering dead bodies gets complicated. Finding out who did it and looking for clues is exciting, but it's dangerous too. Let's call the police and let them deal with this."

"Of course, sure. I wasn't saying I was going to solve it but... Hey, hang on, I know you. You're that guy who was in the paper the other day! You helped solve that thing about the body in a tent and some dude stuffed into a cave or something. And your dog was chewing on a lady's leg in the picture. That's you, right? So cool."

"Yes, that was us. We just got mixed up in it."

"So you have experience? Are you a detective?"

"Me? No, I'm just an ex-chef trying to enjoy vanlife."

"Then this is your lucky day, Max."

"How so?" I asked, genuinely intrigued.

"Because I'm a vanlife guy too. Hashtag vanlife," he said, although I had no idea why. "There are a few of us just up over there." He pointed to the west at a distant field that offered direct access to the beach after crossing the road. Various campervans, cars, and other vehicles were stationed, along with tents and what looked like a large bus. "A few travellers stay here for the summer, plenty move around and only stop for a night or two, and some of us have been here for years. It's very cool."

"Sounds nice. But can you call the police and let them know what's happening? We need to get them here so they can deal with it."

"Sure," he grinned, excited that the monotony had been broken.

I wasn't quite as thrilled.

But then, there was no denying it was rather intriguing and most mysterious.

Chapter 2

Trev and I hung around getting hot and sweaty until the police arrived less than ten minutes later. Two constables were the first on the scene, incongruous in their stiff uniforms when everyone else was naked bar a few flimsy pieces of cloth.

"Guys, over here!" shouted Trev, waving happily as the officers scanned the beach.

"Stop shouting," I warned. "You'll have loads of people coming over to be nosy."

"They'll be over soon enough anyway," he shrugged, unable to hide his excitement.

The officers changed direction and headed our way, looking flustered as the heat reflected off the sand. I explained what I'd found, how Anxious had dug at the sand, and that the foot had toppled. Both were smiling to start with, thinking this was a joke, especially because Trev was hopping about like a kid about to get an ice-cream, but when we stepped aside and revealed the foot, things turned very serious, very quickly. Within minutes, we found ourselves on the other side of a cordon with crime scene tape in a wide area around the foot, secured by pieces of driftwood Trev and I helped the officers place.

The crime was called in and after answering the same questions several times and giving our details, two detectives arrived, both looking familiar the closer they got.

"Not you again," grumbled the man I recalled was named Malcolm. A man so nondescript I would never have been able to describe him.

His partner, on the other hand, was utterly memorable. Short of stature, wide of girth, she was tattooed, with bleached-blond hair in need of a touch-up and a tent of a dress in flamboyant colours—my mind kept conjuring images of a parrot in serious need of a diet change.

"You seem to be making a habit of this," noted Julia warmly, but with her thickly drawn eyebrows raised.

"Trust me, it's not on purpose. I didn't think you would be working here? Don't detectives just cover the local area?"

"In case you hadn't noticed, Max, this is local. We don't get many bodies piling up in the coastal towns of North Wales."

"Not until he came along," grunted Malc as he stepped to the side then ducked under the barrier tape. "Bloody hippies."

"I'm not a hippy," I protested. "Although, maybe I am."

"You look like one. Long hair, big beard, cutoffs, and a vest. Hippy."

"Is that a bad thing?" I asked Malc, genuinely wanting to know.

"Yes."

"Ignore him. He's just jealous because he'd love to be free like you, Max. But he can't be, because he's got a wife and two kids and a stupidly large mortgage."

"You have a wife and children, Malc?" I asked, surprised for some reason. Maybe because I couldn't imagine anyone remembering what he looked like, which would make being married to him difficult. You'd freak out every time you sat down for dinner, and who'd get the remote control?

"Yes. What's so shocking about that?" he huffed, affronted. "And it's DI Anderson to you. My partner is DI Bennet, not Julia. We aren't buddies, we won't be going to the pub, and we'll never start arranging barbecues."

"Chill out, Malc. Sheesh! It's because Max here is thinking the same thing everyone does. How could this boring, forgettable man have a wife when she'd never remember what he looked like?" laughed Julia, punching Malc on the arm playfully.

He winced, then scowled at her.

"Guess this is your lucky day, eh?" smiled Julia as she grabbed my arm and dragged me under the tape towards the foot. "Show me all the gory details."

"Am I supposed to be here?" I asked.

"Bit late for that. You already messed everything up and contaminated the scene."

"So did I," shouted Trev, then lifted the tape and tagged along.

"Hey, you, back on the other side!" ordered Malc.

Trev sulked, but Julia tutted and said, "Stop being such a grump, Malc."

"I keep telling you, it's Malcolm, not Malc."

"Let the youngster tag along. He was the second on the scene and we need to talk to him. Thank you, officers," she said, turning to the two constables. "Anything to report?"

They spent a few minutes talking, going over what we'd told them, then moved to control the growing crowd now gathering to see what the fuss was about.

Malc and Julia drew us close and we grouped around the foot laying in the sand like a cheap prop from a movie. We used our bodies as shields from both the sun and the inquisitive, then stared down at it.

"It's a foot," said Malc, bending.

"A male foot," added Julia. "Been here hours judging by the sunburn. Smells funky too. Got a pen, Malc?"

"You are not poking that foot with my nice pen!" he huffed.

"It's a bloody Biro. They cost ten pence."

"Then use your own."

Julia winked at us, then huffed and puffed as she squatted. Trev and I joined the detectives and peered at the foot like it might suddenly start doing something interesting.

Suddenly, it toppled as the sand shifted, causing us to jump and Anxious to bark at it, his hackles raised.

"It's okay. It won't come after you," I soothed, stroking his head.

Anxious lay down, nose close to the offending toes, eyes locked on.

"You did good work last week," said Julia, not looking at me.

"Showed us up," grunted Malc.

"I didn't mean to interfere," I said. "Things just happened. Everything clicked into place and I wanted to help out Bethan. She's a good officer and wants to get ahead."

"She's a credit to the force," said Julia. "She's being treated with more respect now."

"That's great. Give her my best."

"We aren't your answering service, Max. That's what phones are for," she said, her fierce brown eyes pinned on me.

"Yes, of course. So, what do you think?"

"I think it's a foot on the beach," she stated, matter-of-fact. "I think you need to leave us to deal with this. And I think you need to step away, no pun intended, and not interfere this time."

"Hey, this guy solved a double murder," protested Trev.

"It wasn't like that," I said, shaking my head at him to stop winding the detectives up.

"Yes, it was," he continued, oblivious. "I read all about it. You and that hot policewoman got the bad guys and saved the day. It was awesome. Mickey and Sue are up at the campsite and they told everyone."

"They're here?" I asked, not surprised as they'd said they were travelling along the coast the same as me.

"You should come over, say hi to people and tell us some stories."

"Maybe I will," I grinned.

"When you two have finished making your date, do you think you could leave the detectives to continue their work?" snapped Julia.

"Sorry, ma'am," said Trev with a wink.

"Less of the ma'am. I'm not your granny. You two can get lost now. The officers took your statements and details, I assume?"

We agreed they had, so moved to leave. With a grunt, Julia stood and gave me a card with her contact details. "Just in case you," and she air-quoted, "'find' any clues."

"I'm not involved."

"You weren't involved last time, but you still kept finding bodies and important details. Keep it, just in case. I like you, Max, but less of the 'effort,' okay?" She laughed deep and loud at her own joke. I'd heard every single variation there was regarding my name, and found hers about as amusing as all the others.

With a nod, Trev and I left them to it and walked back towards the lifeguard lookout point.

"What was she laughing at?" asked Trev.

"It's because of my name. Max Effort."

"What is?" he asked, confused.

"That's my name. Max Effort."

"Seriously? I assumed it was a typo in the paper or something. Damn, dude, do you hate your parents?"

"Like you wouldn't believe," I grumbled, when the truth was they were great, if utterly nightmarish, because they were so oblivious to the major faux pas they'd inconvenienced me with.

"So, what now?"

"How'd you mean?" I asked, studying this young man in his twenties with a perfect body, perfect tan, and even perfect hair. He had perfect teeth too. Trev jiggled his pecs, clearly something he did a lot, and I couldn't help chuckle.

"I mean, what do we do to solve this?"

"We do nothing. We leave the police to deal with it. I'm still getting used to my new life on the road, and I need time to settle into things."

"Right, sure," he said, winking. "Off to look for clues, are you?"

"Absolutely not! Solving crimes is exhausting. Although," I moved close and checked nobody was around, adding to the drama for his sake, "it is intriguing, isn't it? Why leave a foot? Why make it look like someone was buried in the sand? Why risk getting caught? And most importantly—"

"Yes?" Trev's eyes were bugging and his cheeks were rosy.

"—where's the rest of the man? Is he dead? Is he still alive? Was there an accident?"

"Maybe a shark did it? I'm always getting loser kids winding me up saying there are sharks, but we do get them here on occasion. Nothing too big, but we get them."

"I think I'll skip on having a swim then." I looked out to sea where people were splashing about, and wondered what would happen when the news spread. Would they all leave, or just get on with their day?

The same as me, I assumed. They'd just carry on. What were you supposed to do after such a thing? Go home and not come back out, or continue with your day?

At this moment, Trev's replacement for the afternoon arrived, so we chatted for a while, filling him in on things. I told them I was going because I'd promised Anxious we could go crabbing and he hated it if I went back on my word. Trev said he knew all the best spots, so would tag along if that was okay. It was. I liked him, and he reminded me of the young man I might have been if life had taken a different turn, or I'd let it. Instead, I'd pursued a career as a fine-dining chef and burned out not only myself but my relationship too. I was making amends, but often thought it was too little, too late. Although, really, it's never too late to admit you got things wrong and start over. That was exactly what I was doing, and so far it wasn't what I'd expected and a lot more exciting than I could have possibly imagined.

We gave the police cordon and the crowd of morbid onlookers a wide berth and strolled along the shoreline towards the rock pools. Trev was a real chatterbox, and very keen to have someone to talk to. I learned that he was in fact twenty-six, not as young as I'd believed, and had been living in his custom van for five years ever since he left college and realised that even with a well-paying job he'd struggle to afford rent, pay bills, and still eat. Instead, he'd opted to pursue his dream of living on the coast and borrowed money from his parents to buy and renovate his van once he secured the lifeguard job.

It meant he not only had a home, but paid his parents back within two years and now had minimal overheads, could live at the beach, be here every day, and had no commute to work. He was a very smart man, and it was no surprise that more and more people were chasing such an existence. Digital nomads, or people with regular jobs who chose this life, the proliferation of people building tiny homes, all were no longer seen as bordering on crazy. They were recognised as people trying to find a better, more balanced and economical way to live. Freed from jobs they hated just to pay a mortgage or ever-rising rent, people now understood how freeing life on the road or in a small building could be, and the world of opportunities it opened was nigh on inexhaustible.

"So, are there others like you at the campsite?" I asked.

"It's not a campsite as such. It's more just a field we're allowed to park or camp in. It's a nominal fee, not like at proper sites, so it's affordable. Most places cost so much, but this lets me live right where I work without it breaking the bank balance. This is just basically someone's big front garden. It belongs to the house up there you can see. It's their field. They own the land and wanted to share the love."

"That's remarkably kind of them. What's in it for them?"

"Their son had a very hard time a decade or so ago. Same position as me where he couldn't afford rent and ended up getting into debt with bad guys and things got nasty. They bailed him out and he moved into an old bus in the field. Then friends heard about it, and then their friends did, and it became a thing around here. His folks are cool, proper old hippy types, and they figured it was a good thing. Tiny homes, vanlife, and travelling are pretty new to most people in this country apart from the gypsies, and we know they have a bad rap. But nowadays it's a sensible thing to do and means people can live a different life."

"I'm beginning to realise that. You're a smart guy, Trev."

"Thanks." He suddenly became coy, but then brightened and pointed ahead. "Look, Anxious, it's the rock pools. Let me show you where to hunt for crabs."

Anxious barked and ran on ahead, keen to warn the crabs he was out for them and no way were they going to nip his nose today.

"Why's he called Anxious?"

"When we first saw him he was an anxious puppy, so it seemed to suit. But then we got the crazy guy home and he was a right terror for a month. He calmed down soon enough, and has been well-behaved ever since, but the name stuck."

"I like it. It suits him somehow." We caught up with the little fella as he stared into a deep pool, body motionless apart from his rear right leg twitching with anticipation as he waited for the crabs to announce themselves. A shoal of tiny fish darted from the shallows and he lost the plot and dove in, barking and splashing, tail slapping against the frothy water.

"He ever catch anything?" asked Trev.

"What do you think?"

The tide had turned and was slowly coming in, so we got down to the serious business of relaxing. Easy to do when you have a deranged dog dreaming of getting one over on a tiny crab, or teaching fish no bigger than his sense a thing or two about life.

Trev knew the expansive area of rock pools intimately, explaining that he'd been coming here ever since he was a baby and it was why he'd chosen to apply for work here. He even had a tale about an old crab that lived in the largest of the pools. A battle-scarred, ferocious beast with one large claw, one small one, and deep gouges in its mature carapace.

We worked our way over to the deep water and waded in, Anxious keeping to the edge where it was shallower. Trev led me to one side and explained this was where the old crab lived. The rocks were high here, easily matching my six foot one. Jagged things covered in mussels and limpets, forming a natural barrier to the tide, ensuring the water flowed in and out slow and steady rather than crashing in and disturbing what was a world within a world of starfish, fish, tiny crabs, and various seaweeds.

Anxious had worked his way around to join us now and stood atop the rocks, towering over us like the lord of the rock pool, yipping with excitement as Trev called out, "Ready?" then began reaching into the water and gently turning over rocks to check for the crab.

I copied him and together we began the hunt. Anxious couldn't help himself and began to bark with excitement, and I turned, distracted as I realised he was no longer watching us but had slipped down the side somewhere to another rock pool.

And then, the most intense pain I had ever felt in my life seared up my arm and I yelped in shock as I yanked my hand from the water to find a monster of a crab hanging onto my thumb.

Our eyes locked, and I knew that from this day on I had made a mortal enemy. The old crab truly was a grizzled specimen, looking like it had fought a daily battle to reach the heady heights as ultimate ruler of the rock pool. Scarred, with chunks missing, its small claw waving menacingly as it held on with its large one and its strange mouth parts opened and closed. Tiny bubbles expanded then popped as it mouthed a silent warning not to come messing in its home.

"Get it off me!" I shouted, waving my arm about in the hopes it would dislodge.

"Looks like you found it," laughed Trev as he waded over and proceeded to do exactly nothing.

"Will it take my thumb off?" I squealed, the pain unbelievably intense. Already my thumb was purple and swelling, and I feared I would lose it.

"Dude, it's not a pair of bolt cutters. It can't chop it off."

"Are you sure?"

"No, not at all," he shrugged, grinning happily.

"How do I get it to let go?"

"Grab its pincer and prize it open. Here, let me show you." Trev carefully took hold of each side of the pincer and eased it loose enough for me to yank my hand back. I hid it behind my back, just in case, and sighed with relief as the crab dropped into the water with a disgruntled splash and scuttled to safety.

"Thanks. I can't believe how much that hurts." I shook my hand out and winced as I peered at my thumb, expecting it to not be there. It was intact, if bruised, and very red, but the colour was easing so I'd managed to survive the encounter relatively unscathed.

"That's what you get for turning over rocks where a giant crab lives," chuckled Trev, wagging a finger at me.

"You said it was how you found him!" I protested.

"I know," he laughed, clearly hoping something like this might happen.

"We're no longer friends," I sulked, then grinned and shook my head.

Anxious was still barking, but he'd missed out on all the "fun" so we clambered out of the water and over the rocks to see what trouble he'd got into now.

We stood on the jagged high stones, our balance precarious as we looked down on Anxious.

"I think we found who the foot belongs to," I said, noting the absence of a foot beneath the torn jeans of a pale man. Anxious tugged at a trouser leg, but failed to drag the corpse from the encroaching tide.

Chapter 3

My head swam with visions of torn clothes and crabs, and I had to grab hold of Trev to steady myself. It was a bad idea, as he was currently bent over double and urging.

Instead, I shook it off, refused to look, and turned Trev away then guided him down off the rocks. After I whistled for Anxious, I helped Trev onto the sand where he slumped and sat with his legs out in front, shoulders hunched.

"You okay? I need to go get the detectives."

"I'm fine. It's just... he was..."

"I know. Wait here, and stay sitting."

Trev nodded mutely, so I left him there and raced back across the beach to the scene where more officers, what looked like forensics specialists, and others were busy doing whatever it was they did.

I gasped to a stop in front of Julia who was busy giving an officer instructions. She spotted me, frowned, then finished talking and took my arm and moved me away from the crowd.

"Let me guess. You found another body, didn't you? Max, this is becoming a very annoying habit."

"Tell me about it. I just want to play with my dog and eat ice-cream. Instead, I can't seem to go more than a few days without somebody turning up dead."

"I'm assuming, or at least hoping, that you found who the foot belongs to?" Julia hitched up her billowing dress and wafted it around her legs, sighing. "I can't handle this heat. It's not good for ladies with a fuller figure."

"You need linen, or something with less material," I said without thinking.

"Oh, so you're a style guru now, are you, Max? Not only are you a chef and traveller, but now you know fashion as well?" Julia looked me up and down, focus on my Crocs and grubby cutoffs.

"You have a point. I was just saying."

"Well don't. I like what I wear and it suits my size. It's not normally this hot, and I don't usually spend as much time on the beach. That's down to you." She glared at me like it was my fault, then her eyes softened and she put a hand to my shoulder. "You okay? Where is he? I assume it's a he?"

"Yes, a man. Mid-thirties, maybe my age, although I'm not good at stuff like that. He had jeans on, really faded ones, and a green vest. Weirdly, I have the same one. It's from Next."

"What is with you and clothes?" she asked, head cocked.

"Nothing. I don't usually think about it. I thought you'd want a description. He had black hair, and there were crabs..."

"Hey, it's okay. You're doing great, Max. Hold it together and show me where he is. Let me get Malc."

She called him over and explained what had happened, then I led them back over to Trev who hadn't moved. Anxious sat beside him, keeping a lookout.

He jumped up and ran over when he spotted us, then rubbed against Julia and Malc's legs like they were long-lost friends.

"He's so cute," laughed Julia, patting him.

"A real sweetheart," agreed Malc, then turned to me, ignoring Anxious.

"Where's the corpse?"

"This way. Be careful. The rocks are really sharp and slippy. And there's a giant crab around here somewhere too."

"I hate the beach," grumbled DI Julia Bennet.

Malc stopped and turned, frowning. "It's awesome. Sun, sand, sea. People having fun. What's not to like? Seriously?"

"Yes, seriously. It's too hot, the sand is boiling, it gets stuck in your knickers and your crevices, and you find it in bed weeks later. It's impossible to get the salt out of your hair, and you always get burned."

"I don't, because I use sunscreen," said Malc smugly.

"Shut up, Malc," sighed Julia, sweating badly now as we clambered over the rocks, Anxious leading the way.

"Watch yourselves," I warned as we manoeuvred around the sharpest section. I put a hand out to help Julia over and heaved as she pushed off with her legs. Once we were over and down the other side, we were confronted with the body half-submerged by the encroaching tide.

"Bugger," muttered Malc.

"Give us a hand, Max. We need to get him out of here before the tide takes him."

It was the last thing I wanted to do, but I knew it had to be done, so we dropped into the water and I took an arm, Malc took the other, and Julia waded in and grabbed his feet. Okay, one foot, one shin. She didn't even blanch at the gore.

We scuttled sideways like the angry crab across the shoreline as waves lapped at our legs, half dragging, half carrying the man. The load was surprisingly heavy, and the flesh was cold, but I put it out of my mind and just did what needed to be done.

Once out of the water, we dragged him up the beach as far as we could then collapsed, exhausted, onto the sand.

Trev and Anxious came over and he asked, "Need a hand?" with perfect timing. He took one look at the body and turned away. I understood his reticence.

"Just go and get the other officers," grunted Julia through her wheezing, then she flopped onto her back and lay there, panting heavily.

Malc and I were no better, but I remained seated as I tried to get my breath back, refusing to look at the dead man beside me.

Yet again we had to explain our actions, go through what we'd seen, and repeat it several times. But we were finally told we could leave, and this time we did exactly that, beating a hasty retreat up the beach. As we reached the road, I spied a man watching us through binoculars, but he hurried away. Who was that? I recalled the man from Rhyl who'd arrived without a tent and I'd got a strange vibe about, but he hadn't been the killer, just a strange guy who liked to watch people. Barry, that was his name. Volvo Barry. He still wore brown corduroys and a brown shirt that matched his brown car. What was he doing here?

Trev had moved ahead, so I dismissed Barry from my mind and entered the car park where I'd paid for a full day as I'd planned to pick up some choice ingredients for dinner.

"Sweet," gushed Trev as I unlocked the campervan, his stress of earlier seemingly forgotten.

I too felt a calmness wash over me as I opened the side doors of the sixties camper and retro vibes slapped me in the face like a wet tie-dye shirt stinking of patchouli. Home, it was the familiarity of home. Somewhere safe. Somewhere that was mine. My refuge.

"You like it?" I asked, beaming.

"Mate, it's awesome! Look at that interior! Not all of them have kitchens, and certainly not head height if they're this old. Mostly original too. You lucky sod. I love a pop-up roof."

"Thanks. I've been learning more about it, and I know some of it isn't strictly original, but most is. Think the roof's always been like that?"

"Yes, I'm sure. It's different with these old splitties, but it's original. The later models had larger raised roofs as they didn't have all the windows, but at least you can cook in comfort and you have a small section to slide over for a bed, right?"

"Yes, but it isn't very comfortable, and that's definitely a bodge job."

"But it's there in case you need it. I love these old vans. Bet it cost you a fortune."

"More than I expected to pay, but I wanted something with character."

"And you got it. Seriously, dude, come over to the field and stay with us. You'll like it there. Everyone's sound, and it's very cheap."

"Maybe I will. But I've paid for another day, so maybe tomorrow?"

"Yeah, cool. Let me give you my number."

We exchanged contact details then Trev left. I think he was relieved to be heading home after the day we'd had, and I didn't blame him.

This was when I really discovered how awesome it was having my home right here when I needed it. I might have been in a car park at a beach in North Wales, but my home was here. I put the kettle on, made a drink, then sat on the bench seat and stared out of the window at the beach and holidaymakers. Off in the distance, I could see the police going about their business, and several more cars arrived, lights flashing, but for most people it was a fun day out, although for one man it was his last.

How did he lose his foot? Why was it buried like that? Why was he left by the water? So many questions, but no answers. I wondered what the police would discover.

Anxious seemed exhausted by the morning's excitement, and was curled up with his head resting in my lap, sleeping soundlessly. I could have happily joined him, but was too wired after such madness. So I sipped my tea and tried not to think about much of anything at all.

Apart from Min. She'd been on my mind a lot ever since I abandoned my conventional life and embarked on this adventure. The fact she'd shown up the day after I left, along with my parents, then stayed the night after they went home—although there was no cuddling up in bed much to my disappointment—meant she still had real feelings for me, but I couldn't see where it was heading.

During the lead up to the divorce, I had told Min I still loved her and didn't want to part, but things had gone too far, and we were already so distant, that she refused to withdraw the divorce application and I went along with it as it was what she wanted.

Foolish, and a terrible end to our time together, but I had promised I would change, turn my life around, and I had. I gave her the house, bought a crappy one for myself, quit my job, got my act together, and became a better man. I knew the chances of us getting back together were slim, so decided it was time for me to move on and leave her to build a new future for herself.

But now it seemed like me leaving had given her a real jolt, and possibly helped her realise that she did want me in her life. What a mess. All I could do was give her some space, let her figure things out, and to be fair, I had only been gone a matter of days.

Nevertheless, I called and told her what had happened. She was concerned, then excited, then worried, then excited all over again. I promised not to put myself in any danger, and that I wasn't involved like last time when I helped a young police officer follow a trail of clues. Just to be on the safe side, I told her where I was staying, where I would most likely move the campervan to tomorrow, and promised to text her before bedtime so she wouldn't worry.

"Come visit any time you want," I said before I hung up.

"Maybe I will. But I shouldn't really. I don't want to give you any false sense of hope that we're getting back together."

"Min, you don't need to say that. I know we'll get back together at some point. I'm just here waiting for when you feel ready."

"Max, please don't..."

I hung up, feeling smug, and nudged Anxious until he lifted a paw and gave me a high-five.

"Did I say the right thing then?" I asked him. "Think Min wants to come live with us in Vee?"

Anxious' ears pricked up and he barked his agreement.

"Good, then I said the right thing. I will get her back, Anxious. She'll be a part of our future no matter how long it takes. Maybe it will be a year or two, but we're in no hurry. And we're young. You're only three, and I'm only thirty-three. We have our whole future ahead of us."

Anxious snored beside me. Maybe he wasn't as keen as me, or maybe he'd heard it all before. I smiled to myself, knowing I would do whatever I could to make up for past mistakes with Min. Maybe I was pushing things, but she had to know how I felt as at least that way I knew I'd done what I could to put right all the wrongs.

But this was far into the future, I assumed, and I knew I had to get on with my own life too. Which meant...

"Lunchtime!"

Anxious jolted awake, shot up to a sitting position, wagged furiously, licked my beard, stared at me with wide eyes, then jumped from the bench seat and locked his eyes on the fridge, willing the door to open with his Terrier super powers that hadn't quite come to fruition yet but he knew would one day, and soon, and then all the sandwiches would be his.

"It'll happen, buddy. Just keep practising," I laughed.

Anxious snapped his head around to glance at me, then resumed vibing the miniature fridge behind the old cupboard door.

I sorted out the packed lunch I'd made that morning, and we sat in the car park by the beach enjoying ourselves immensely as we tucked into thick crusty bread from a fancy local bakery filled with cheese, tomato chutney, ham, and French Dijon mustard. Anxious wasn't a fan of mustard so I'd made him one without, but I got the feeling he would have eaten mine given half the chance.

Once lunch was over, I made another cup of tea just because I could, and felt smug about it, too, then even turned a small fan on and let the cool air wash over us as we sat and watched the world go by.

"How about an ice-cream?" I suggested. "I'm not going to make a habit out of it, or we'll both get fat, and we aren't really on holiday. We just live like this now. But as a treat?"

Anxious most likely didn't understand this new life, and I wanted to ensure he settled into it, so a treat would help with that, but I suspected the little fella would have been happy wherever we were as long as we remained together. We'd been inseparable ever since Min and I got him as he came to work with me, and I couldn't imagine life without him by my side.

With my pooch pinned to my leg, keeping a watchful eye on me in case I decided to sprint off and eat all the ice-cream, I locked up and weaved through the packed car park. How were there so many people here on a work day? It wasn't the school holidays or a Bank Holiday, and yet it was rammed. I supposed it was the weather. Us Brits needed to make the most of it whenever we could, and the heatwave was bringing everyone out.

Most people were actually either of retirement age, with young children, or I supposed taking holiday days, but it was still rather strange seeing just how many tourists were here. Was there an event? We made it to the high street, a typical seaside arrangement with the main drag running parallel to the shore so the biggest houses lining the street got great views. Most were Victorian, three-storey, painted in bright colours as was tradition. At least half were bed-and-breakfast places where you could rent a room for a night or two at a reasonable cost and get a hearty fry-up thrown in for good measure. Usually run by the owners, these places were warm, welcoming, and beat a faceless hotel any day. Plus, you got to be right by the beach.

We paused to check out the shops, Anxious only interested in balls and frisbees, and I made a mental note of the fish and chip shop, a cafe, and several others I'd missed when we'd arrived. After a few days here, I was becoming familiar with the town, but we hadn't spent much time on the main road as it was mostly food we'd been after so we'd been to Pensarn and Abergele, the small town that gave Abergele Beach its name.

The most popular ice-cream shop was at the end of the road at the beginning of town and apparently had some of the best in the country. Made with local milk from a farm up the road, with local ingredients, and no doubt made by local people, everyone I'd spoken to raved about it and how fair the price was and how generous the portions. Apparently, there was a secret ingredient known only to the owner that he added to the mix every morning, and it meant the ice-cream couldn't be beaten.

"I heard," I confided to Anxious, "you get two scoops in a waffle cone and you can have free sprinkles or sauce if you want. Do you want sprinkles or sauce?"

Anxious barked happily.

"Sprinkles it is," I laughed, smiling down at him.

I looked ahead, expecting a large queue, but instead what I found was a crowd spread out into the road holding up traffic, three police cars, a cordon, and if I wasn't mistaken wasn't that DI's Bennet and Anderson sitting in the unmarked car?

"What now?" I wondered. "Looks like ice-cream's off the menu."

Anxious whined, but tugged on the lead, optimistic as always.

In the confusion, I lost my grip, not expecting him to react this way as it was very out of character, and he raced ahead between the legs of the crowd then was gone.

Chapter 4

"Anxious!" I hollered, my voice drowned out by the crowd surging forward to see what was happening.

People tutted as I squeezed between them, but it wasn't exactly a mob as this was tourist central and they just craved ice-cream. I made it to the barrier tape soon enough. A small area sectioned off around the entrance to the shop, but what looked like little more than a kiosk really. Ice-cream was on display behind a glass-fronted freezer, but there was next to nothing in any of the numerous tubs and only a single officer inside standing beside a woman sitting in a chair, crying.

I searched for Anxious but still couldn't see him, just people being nosy and several officers behind the tape telling everyone to stay back and that there was nothing to see.

Stressed about the little guy as he wasn't great with crowds and could get disoriented, I eased to the side and into the road, figuring I could grab him if he ran into traffic without realising. The frustrated constable gave everyone strict instructions to leave, so slowly the crowd dispersed, clearing the way for the car that now pulled up outside. Detectives Malc and Julia got out and scowled at the people grumbling as they walked off, muttering about not getting any ice-cream. They spied me and looked less than happy. The DIs exchanged a few words then came over to me as

Anxious bolted from the shop with an officer shouting at him; I bent and scooped him up before he caused any trouble.

"You sneaky thief," I couldn't help laughing, as he had a waffle cone wedged between his teeth, and looked guilty as hell.

Anxious wagged happily and scrambled to get free when he saw Julia.

"He likes you," I said, grinning, then let him down.

"And I like him. But he shouldn't be loose here. This is a crime scene."

"Sorry, I didn't know. I lost my grip on his lead. I was just coming to get an ice-cream." Anxious barked. "Make that two ice-creams."

"This is getting annoying," grumbled Malc as he glowered. "What are you doing here, Mr. Effort? Are you listening in on our radios?"

"What? No, of course not. Can you even do that?"

"Get him out of here, Julia," he hissed, then with a final glare at me he ducked under the tape and entered the shop.

"Ignore him. Grumpy is his default setting," said Julia, smiling wearily as she wiped the sweat from her brow with a handkerchief.

"That's okay. So what's going on? Not another murder?"

"No, not another one. We confirmed the victim's identity. He's well-known around here. He owns, runs, and makes the ice-cream for this place. Apparently, it's the best in North Wales and very popular. He lives upstairs in a flat. The one with the balcony, see?"

I craned my neck to see a wide, ornate Victorian balcony festooned with pot plants, pelargoniums spilling crimson joy down the railings.

"That's good you know who he is. So why all the fuss here? To check for clues?"

"We got a call from the woman inside. She was worried as the victim hadn't been seen since first thing this morning. That's his girlfriend and business partner. She said he got up at four like he always does to go make the ice-cream but he never returned. She was worried they'd run out, but after he was a no-show and she couldn't get an answer from him she sent one of the staff to check where he makes the ice-cream and the place was an utter disaster."

"What was it like?"

"Max, you're a decent guy and I like you, but I'm not here to answer your questions. You found him, sure, but this doesn't involve you. Can you please leave this well alone and let us do our job? Last week you lucked out and stumbled across a few clues, but this is different. We have leads, clues, suspects, and it's dangerous. Do I make myself clear? Things aren't as they seem. You don't know who you're dealing with, and in case you've forgotten, the victim had his foot amputated. It wouldn't have been done in a nice way with anaesthetic and a sharp saw. It was... Anyway, understand? Leave this alone."

"I will, don't you worry. You're right, last time I was in the right place at the right time, and found some clues, and things clicked, but you have to admit I'm pretty good at figuring stuff out. I treat it like my cooking."

Clearly intrigued despite her desire to see the back of me, Julia turned with raised eyebrows and asked, "How so?"

"A lot goes into making a dish worthy of a Michelin 3-star restaurant. There's so much planning, you need the best ingredients, and you need endless patience."

"Get on with it, Max. I haven't got all day."

"Bear with me. But what's most important of all is the detail. You have to have a real eye for things. It's not enough to just be a great chef. You have to look for tiny imperfections, little clues as to what works and what doesn't. There's a fine balance. That's why I was so good at figuring out those deaths last week. I saw things neither you, Malc, nor anyone else saw. Admit it."

"Fine, you're right, and it rankles."

"So it wasn't just luck. My mind is analytical and creative. I notice the details even if my conscious mind doesn't register it right away. I returned to the cottage, I remembered the stains, I put the pieces together. So did Bethan. I'm not for one minute saying you wouldn't have figured it out, but you know it goes beyond me just being lucky."

"Okay, yes, you got me. You did well and we were very impressed. But, Max, this is different, okay? Trust me on this. You don't want to get involved. Leave me and Malc to deal with things, and do not get in our way. Malc is already pissed at you. I warn you now, he may seem like a boring guy, but if you get on his wrong side he'll come down on you like a ton of bricks. Are we clear?"

"Sure, I understand. And look, I really did just come to get ice-cream."

"Then go somewhere else to get it. This shop is closed for the foreseeable future. Now, I have to go talk to a grieving woman. See you around, Max. But not too soon, I hope."

"See you around."

With a nod, Julia turned and spoke to an officer. He lifted the barrier tape for her and she ducked under then huffed her way up the steps, clearly struggling with the heat which was now becoming almost intolerable.

Anxious had finished his cone long ago and was pining for the real thing, so we hunted around until we found another place called Lovely Stuff. We had a rather average ice-cream served by a guy who was so grumpy he didn't even bother gossiping about the extra business he was getting, and then I decided to call it quits and pick up the ingredients for our one-pot wonder this evening.

By the time we'd finished shopping, it was mid-afternoon and I'd had more than enough of the town so headed back along the coast road then took the turn onto a winding lane and once again prayed there would be nobody coming the other way. I made it without incident, and performed a task I was getting more and more used to and hopped out, opened the farm gate, drove through, got out again and closed it, then drove to my spot.

Canny vanlife expert that I now was after a week living this way, I'd left not only my camping chair but a sun shelter at my spot so nobody would take the prime piece of real estate I'd managed to nab. Not that I'd needed it here, as for some reason it was utterly empty bar a single man in the bottom corner of the field. I couldn't figure it out, but when I'd spoken to the owner that morning he'd said it was usual for this time of the year, but in a few weeks business picked up dramatically and they were usually full until September.

I didn't mind one bit, as the peace was perfect.

We were surrounded on all sides by woodland, making the campsite cool and comfortable. There were no sea views, but what there was instead made up for it. Dark, brooding Welsh hills covered in bracken and heather made for a colourful patchwork of browns, greens, and gold with tough sheep grazing happily on the steep sides.

The campsite field was mown short, bright and verdant with the damp air that got trapped here every morning, so before I did anything I just slumped into my chair and soaked up the silence.

Anxious spread himself out on the grass, shoving with his feet to rub against the ground, then rolled onto his back and did that weird thing many dogs do and pumped his legs into the air while he grinned with pleasure. It always brought a smile to my face.

After a suitable rest to recharge my batteries, I busied myself in my kitchen/living room/bedroom/means of transport, whistling happily as I put my insanely heavy cast-iron pot onto the two-ring hob to heat through slowly. With butter added, I seared the meat, a lovely piece of rump, then threw in a few cloves of garlic, and generally felt happy with the world as the smells built and my stomach rumbled. Once all the ingredients had been fried and the stock added, I put the lid on, turned the heat right down, and left the pot to its own devices for a few hours.

One thing I'd learned over the years is that the best dishes take time. You simply cannot rush these things. It's tempting to cut times short, but the flavour difference is incredible, so I resigned myself to a long wait better to enjoy the meal and truly make it a feast fit for two kings.

Yet again, I pottered around in the campervan as was my daily routine now. Tidying, organising, coming up with new and ingenious ways to maximise space and to run an audit on what I needed or could give away. It had been a steep learning curve so far, with numerous adjustments having to be made to my life, from the amount of crockery I owned, to simple things like spatulas, knives, chopping boards, and even cleaning products. They all took up space, and that was one thing I didn't have much of.

So far, clothes hadn't been such an issue as I'd left winter coats and other items with my parents, but come winter I wondered where it would all go. I guess I'd cross that bridge when I came to it.

It was only once the smell of dinner hit me that I realised my mistake as I'd yet again put the pot on to cook inside when I had a portable camping stove I could have used outside and saved the smells in the van. Plus, I would have had more room. It was half the reason why I'd bought the shelter. I could have a lovely outdoor kitchen using the fold-out table, and not worry about grease marks or having to clean up the van.

"Next time, Max. Don't forget," I reminded myself. But I wasn't stressed. I was calm, happy, and enjoying myself immensely.

With everything spick and span, I relaxed into my chair once again and let my mind drift where I knew it inevitably would. To the beach and the sight of the foot, then the body of the man in the rock pools. I hoped Trev was okay as he was shaken by the sights, but I couldn't help wondering what had happened to the man who made ice-cream for a living. Why would someone kill him in such a gruesome way? Why ransack the place he made the ice-cream? And where was that? Why wasn't it on the premises where they sold it?

I was, I knew, a nosy sod at times, and it wasn't always appreciated. British custom was to mind your own business, not ask questions, and mostly pretend like nothing was wrong even when it was. But I wasn't like that, never had been. Mum and Dad always said that ever since I could speak I was inquisitive, wanting to know how things worked, why, and never tired of learning. It was why I made such a great chef, but there was a dark side to my nature, and I knew that as well as them. Just like Min did.

Such things can become obsessive, and I was an obsessive. Once I got interested in a topic, I was like a dog with a bone and refused to let go, wanting to know all there was to know. It meant I was a single-minded chef, as good is it got. But as every obsessive knew, when you focused that much on one aspect of your life, everything else suffered. It was inevitable.

Was I going to look into this strange slaughter at the seaside?

Of course I was!

More out of curiosity than anything, I wanted to know why the man was dead, but I had to admit it had given me a sense of satisfaction to help solve the crimes committed the previous week, and maybe I wanted more of that. But what I had told Julia was also true. I had a keen eye for detail and it had been invaluable. Maybe I could help, no matter what she and her partner had said.

Tomorrow might bring new insights, but for today I was done with thoughts of murder and feet, so focused on dinner, and once it was ready and Anxious was champing at the bit, I served us both a generous bowl and sat in my chair as heaven on a spoon was delivered to my taste buds in a burst of glory worthy of the ingredients I'd carefully selected.

With full stomachs, and the bed already made in advance—I was learning—we hit the hay relatively early, both exhausted from our day.

We slept like babies, not waking until the dawn broke. I groaned as I looked at the clock. Half four! I'd forgotten to draw the curtains yet again. There really was more to this vanlife than anyone could possibly imagine.

When I opened the door to the outside and looked at where I was, I smiled. It might be early, but who wants to sleep when they live in paradise?

Anxious yawned from the bed, showing little inclination to leave his snug spot, so I left the door open and stepped out onto the wet grass after slipping on my Crocs. Birds were busy already, a welcome dawn chorus, but the sun was yet to rise over the high hills behind me, leaving the air with a definite chill that I knew I'd be craving in a few hours.

Making the most of the early morning, I made coffee outside then just sat and enjoyed myself, wondering what Min was doing, if she was asleep, then cursing myself for letting my thoughts drift to her again.

After morning ablutions, I gave Anxious his dog food, had a small bowl of overnight oats, then cleared everything away and tackled the gazebo. Some called them sun shelters, and I was never sure of the correct term. I supposed at this time of the year it was a sun shelter but could just as easily be a rain shelter. It came down quicker than it had gone up, and in no time we were good to go.

Taking Trev up on his offer seemed like a good idea, not that he owned the place or anything, so I weaved through the lanes, hit the open road at the coast, and arrived ten minutes later only to realise it was still an ungodly hour and there was no way anyone would be up yet.

I was mistaken, and it seemed like several people were already leaving in their campervans, and there were several hikers packing tiny one-man tents ready for a long day presumably following the route that you could walk around the entire coastline of Wales. The campsite, or whatever they called it, had separate access to the house up the hill with a hedge between but there was no cabin or reception where I should pay so I stopped a guy with a huge pack on his shoulders and asked what the deal was. He said the owner would be around at some point, you never knew when, to take payment, but it was very relaxed here and I could just pitch up wherever I wanted.

Taking a moment to scope things out, I found a lovely spot with incredible views right down at the bottom by the road that bisected the land from the beach the other side, so decided to park there. I couldn't fathom why such prime real estate hadn't been taken already, so felt quite smug as I got out and Anxious joined me to admire the view.

A new day. A new adventure. A new home within a home.

Chapter 5

The campsite definitely had a hippy vibe, with motorhomes and campervans of all shapes, sizes, age, and price. This was a mixed bag where some people were obviously living in luxury with motorhomes almost as large as regular houses, while there were plenty of basic vans that showed no sign of being converted to tiny living accommodation. I'd been seeing more and more of them now I knew what to look out for, and was rather shocked by just how many had chosen this way of life. When I'd looked it up online, I was incredulous at discovering an estimated half a million people lived in vans, motorhomes, static caravans and the like, and I felt certain there were many more that hadn't been reported.

Now I spotted vehicles with telltale signs everywhere. A solar panel on the roof, movement in the back, or maybe curtains at windows. It ranged from miniature vehicles not much bigger than cars, right up to old buses and everything in between.

Here, we had examples of almost all the numerous options. I loved it immediately.

"Sanctuary" was the rather pretentious name for the site. It brought up memories of a TV show and I was dubious about the choice but I supposed it fit, especially when you took the history of the site into consideration.

One man's sanctuary from the stress of rent or a mortgage, then offered to others, it truly was a lifeline for many.

I got set up with the van and the sun shelter, my chair, and decided to spend some time sorting out a proper kitchen under the cover. Once finished, I stepped back proudly and nodded my approval. With the hob on the table, pots and pans, a box full of crockery and cutlery, drinks, food items, and with space left over, it was a real luxury. I vowed to take the time to get prepared this way from now on, weather permitting, if I was staying at places for more than a day or two.

Checking out how others had arranged their pitches, I realised this was actually standard practice, with some going as far as having makeshift sofas from pallets and cushions, or blow-up versions which looked utterly uncomfortable and not very dog friendly. I secured the wind break, too, another staple of seasoned travellers, and noticed the difference immediately. The breeze lessened, the sun shelter was more stable, and I'd be able to use the kettle without the flame extinguishing half the time.

Things were looking up, so I made a celebratory cuppa then sank into my chair, smug and content, as others emerged from their homes to the raucous sound of doors sliding open and banging shut, sleepy groans, and more farting than I was used to, even though I slept with Anxious every night. Slowly, the site came to life in all its multicoloured, disparate glory.

Unable to take my eyes off things, I watched in wonder at the different ways people readied for their day. Some clearly lived and stayed here. I assumed many were digital nomads, having found work online to bring the money in, while others were pensioners and looked the happiest of all. There were crusty types with long dreadlocks, and those with traditional music festival clothes that looked more like rag rugs.

But more astonishing were the number of people who hurried from their vehicles and raced to the shower blocks then emerged looking smart, professional, and ready to battle their way through another gruelling day. Office workers, men in suits, delivery drivers, all the jobs you could think of. This way of living went beyond young vanlife enthusiasts looking to save on rent. It was a way of life for many, and for all manner of reasons.

This is not to say that the place was rammed and everyone was living on top of their neighbours. The field was huge, the residents numbering maybe a hundred spread out over several acres, but it was truly fascinating and opened my eyes to the world I was now at least a tentative part of.

I spied Trev and waved, and he changed direction and came down to say hello. He still only wore his red shorts, and I realised that must be his thing.

"You made it then?" he beamed. "You'll have people all over you soon enough. Everyone loves an old VW."

"So I'm beginning to learn. Thanks for the heads-up about this place."

"My pleasure."

"How are you doing after yesterday? And did you know it was the guy who runs the ice-cream shop?"

"Not at the time. I didn't recognise him because, to be honest, I didn't look at his face as I was grossed-out enough already."

"I was at the ice-cream shop and spoke to the DIs. He lived there? Had a girlfriend? But didn't he make the ice-cream on the premises? The police said it was trashed."

"That's news to me. About it being trashed, I mean. I know where he made it though. He had a place just down the road where he could work in peace. He was a real artisan, took it very seriously. But why do you want to know?" I rubbed at my beard and his eyes lit up. "You want to solve it! You do, don't you?"

"Maybe a little," I admitted. "I'm curious, is all. You can't tell me you aren't? A foot chopped off, an ice-cream maker dead. His factory trashed. What gives?"

"Look, Max, you're a nice guy and I like you, but you should stay out of this." Trev checked nobody was eavesdropping but moved closer anyway. "The dead dude, Simon, was a real character around the area. Everyone knew him, and he was just one of those guys. A face, if you know what I mean?"

"Grew up here? Knew the locals?" I asked, not understanding.

"More than that. A regular at the pubs, knew the other geezers, got into bother now and then. He never went to jail or anything like that, but he couldn't help being a bit dodgy. A lovable rogue is how I think your generation call guys like that."

"Hey, I'm only seven years older than you!"

"And when you were my age, I was nineteen. And when you were nineteen, I was twelve," he ribbed, smiling.

"Fair point. Dodgy, is what I'd call it."

"Yeah, exactly. He knew people, if you get my drift. Not my thing at all. I'm pretty straight, and don't mess with criminals. I want a quiet life and to surf and enjoy the beach. But Simon's different. Yes, he set up his business making and selling ice-cream, and has been with his partner Lucy for years, but he was also a character, and a troubling one. If he got his foot chopped off, he obviously said something to someone and they weren't happy, so why on earth would you want to get mixed up in that? Keep your head down and stay clear, Max, if you know what's good for you."

"You might be right," I conceded. "I certainly like my feet."

"Me too. So don't go poking your nose in."

"Okay, sure. So, you heading to work?"

"Yeah, and for once I'm hoping nothing exciting happens," he said glumly.

"That's the spirit," I laughed, slapping him on the back. "Hey, mind if I tag along for a while? Anxious needs his W word, so I want to take him to the beach."

"A walk?"

"No, don't say it!"

Anxious yipped, shot up and out of the campervan, and raced around our legs. If he knew where the lead was, I felt certain he'd go get it.

"Sorry, I didn't think," spluttered Trev, bemused. "I'll be back in a few minutes, then we can go. And Max?"

"Yes?"

"You aren't tagging along so you can get me to show you where Simon made the ice-cream, are you?"

"Why would you think that?" I asked innocently.

"Because I'm beginning to realise that whatever I say you're going to look into this. Why?"

"That's a good question, and the honest answer is that because these things keep happening when I'm around, it feels like it's my duty to help. As though this is the reason why I'm living like this. I hope that makes sense?"

"I guess. Okay, Max, sure, but it's your funeral. Don't say I didn't warn you."

I locked up with Anxious going crazy, but Trev was true to his word and returned in a few minutes so we crossed the field, went through a small gate for pedestrians, and were on the pavement across the road from the beach.

"How cool is this?" he beamed.

"It's not exactly a long commute," I laughed. "You have it made. What do you do in the winter?"

"I work at the swimming pool at the leisure centre, volunteer for the RNLI so I get to go on boats, and bits and bobs to keep the money coming in. But I also do a lot of surfing. Wouldn't change it for the world."

"I bet. Come on, show me around for a while before you start work. If that's okay?"

"Sure, but like I said, this is a bad idea."

We skirted the beach then turned off at a junction and weaved our way up a hill past shops and houses, a real mishmash of Victorian properties, modern additions, more conservatories than I'd ever seen in one place in my life, and ancient Welsh stone cottages with high walls to block the winter storms, until we came to a series of small industrial buildings. Most had seen better days, and were shuttered, no signs outside, but several were freshly painted, had vehicles with branded decals, and staff arriving. Large trucks were outside a few, either being loaded or making deliveries.

"That's Simon's there." Trev pointed to the unmistakable ice-cream factory with a large sign above the roller shutter doors.

"Made by Mavis?" I read, turning to Trev.

"Yeah, there's a story behind it. Apparently, that's Simon's mum's name. He got the first few recipes from her, plus the secret recipe, and they were in business together way back when. She was old and more just a face, but people loved her around here and she'd been making ice-cream for decades. They were a right pair, and a good team, but she passed a long time ago. Simon built the business up and kept the name. Good branding."

"I bet. I assume the woman on the sign is his mum?"

"Sure is. Sweet old lady smiling, bright colours, a happy cow. What's not to like? The milk's from just up the road, and all the ingredients too. Real local business."

"So I heard. How does it work then? Do they get the milk, cream, and eggs delivered then make ice-cream?"

"I guess." Trev shrugged. "All I know is it's the best, but I haven't got a clue how it's made."

"Thanks for showing me."

"No problem, but let's get out of here. I don't want anyone seeing us."

I nodded in agreement, so we wandered back to the beach and once on the sand I let Anxious off the lead and he tore away, happy to stretch his legs and just enjoy life. After saying goodbye to Trev, I threw the ball for a while as we walked along the shoreline, greeting walkers or those exercising their dogs, and we had a very pleasant hour just doing nothing much at all.

I couldn't get the factory out of my mind, though, and wondered what state it was in. Why would it be ransacked? Why was it a target? Why Simon? It bugged me, I have to admit. I couldn't understand why a man's foot would be chopped off and he'd be dumped on the beach.

Walk over, much to Anxious' disgust, we returned to the road then retraced our steps back to the factory. It was quiet outside the other businesses now, so I took a gamble and crossed over the yard to the Made by Mavis factory.

I was shocked to find that the tape across the open entrance was hanging to one side, assuming the shutters would have been pulled down and locked. Maybe the police were inside? I doubted it, as there was no car, so why was it open?

Anxious barked, then ran into the dark interior. I cursed silently then glanced around before following, phone in hand and the emergency services already dialled in just in case I was being the right level of paranoid. All I had to do was hit send, assuming I still had my hands.

I stood at the loading bay and let my eyes adjust, which didn't take long as there were skylights inside and the day was bright. The factory was smaller than I'd expected from the outside, crammed with machines, long metal benches familiar from the kitchens I'd worked in, with other industrial touches like sinks, fridges, and freezers. An office was at the rear taking up a third of the space, along with a bathroom, a break room, and a large walk-in freezer.

The machines for making ice-cream were huge, monstrous things with massive metal vats and churns that could easily have your arm off if you weren't careful. Or your foot! They were like cement mixers but much cleaner, and I wondered how the entire process worked on such a large scale and how much was produced here every day.

Much of the equipment was either toppled or damaged in some way. Either broken by a sledgehammer was my guess, or just thrown into the middle where a pile of broken parts now lay like a funeral pyre to the joys of a cold treat on a warm day.

But why?

Anxious looked up at me and cocked his head, tail wagging as he waited for my word. I preferred to think of most things I said to him as a suggestion, but there was no denying that however smart he was sometimes there had to be a command so he knew where he stood in the world, which was being awesome!

"Go find a clue," I suggested, and he was off, zig-zagging this way and that, nose to the ground, tail spinning, licking up any tasty treats he found as he tracked scents the human nose could never uncover.

My assumption was that the place had already been fingerprinted and thoroughly inspected, confirmed by the traces of white residue on much of the damaged equipment, but same as the police would undoubtedly be, I was certain that whoever had done this would have worn gloves.

The ice-cream churns were of most interest, and I focused my attention on them. I understood the mechanics, the need for a slow, steady mix over an extended period, and they were, or had been, in excellent condition. Simon had clearly been at the early stages of his day's work when this act of pointless vandalism occurred, with only a few machines in use, still dripping sticky, sweet-smelling residue all over the floor. Large puddles of milk had soaked through bags of sugar, causing the bottoms to split and piles of sweet goodness to spread out like sandcastles ruined by the encroaching tide. Bottles and jars of colouring and fresh fruit were smashed to the ground in what looked like a fit of rage, but there was no sign of blood, certainly no handy saw or cleaver with which to separate a man from his foot.

It was almost as though he'd left his work and never returned. Why would that be?

Along one wall dull metal milk urns remained lined up, silent witnesses to the violence, those nearest the door empty, those further into the factory still full judging by the weight. Shouldn't it be refrigerated? Maybe it was about to be used? Why hadn't it been touched? Had the milkman delivered today? That would be a regular morning activity and Lifeguard Trev said it was from just up the road, so maybe the dairy farmer had seen something.

With Anxious still having nothing to report, I pushed open the office door with my foot and stepped inside. It was puzzling because the room wasn't disrupted in any way. It was an old-fashioned space with a brown filing cabinet, a whiteboard full of scratchy writing noting the production schedule for the week, which was an eye-opener as making ice-cream required long hours and very early starts. A cheap desk took up much of the remaining space, with a black office chair on one side and two battered green chairs for visitors. The desk itself was rather chaotic, but not enough to appear to have been disturbed. Piles of paperwork were in trays, a keyboard sat alone, cables hanging loose, but there was no computer or monitor. My guess was that it had been taken by the police to check over for any clues. Or it had been stolen.

Maybe that was what they'd come for?

I was pushing my luck, but I rifled through the paperwork, finding nothing of interest, just bills, receipts, random stuff you'd expect for any business, and the drawers were devoid of anything apart from staplers, hole punches, Sellotape, and a half empty bottle of Jack Daniels. No glass. Which was weird.

Anxious came in as I turned to leave, nose going gangbusters as he trailed across the sad grey carpet, then stopped at the filing cabinet and began to whine. He pawed at the bottom drawer, scrabbling like he could climb and reach the summit, then turned and barked once.

"You found something? Good boy." I pulled out a treat from my canvas army surplus satchel I'd bought the day before, finding that this life as a traveller meant I had to carry a fair few things with me at all times and keys, phone, wallet, poo bags, treats, and snacks didn't go well with cutoffs and a vest.

Anxious settled in a corner to take a well-deserved break, so I bent and yanked on the closed drawer, not expecting it to be unlocked, surprised when it was.

There was nothing inside. Absolutely nothing. I checked the other drawers, again unlocked, and again utterly empty. I noticed that the top drawer, where the lock was that secured the whole cabinet, was bent a little, the paint scratched off around the rim, and wondered if this had been forced open. There was a dusting of white around it, and on the other drawers, so I assumed the police had the same idea.

Had this been emptied, or was it simply never used?

I stood, puzzled, and noticed the framed photos and certificates on the yellowing walls. Awards for best ice-cream several years in a row for the county, and other competitions won, hygiene certificates, and a handful of photos of Simon with friends, I assumed. Possibly staff? How many people worked here? He was smiling, and looked almost unrecognisable, as the only other time I'd seen him he'd been lying in the water and very dead.

One photo was of a man I believed to be Simon with three women. All wore white jackets, white Wellington boots, hair nets, and gloves. They were smiling, standing at the open shutter door, so I presumed this was the entire workforce.

Moving to leave, Anxious barked, and I turned to find him back at the filing cabinet, scratching away like before.

"There's nothing there. Sorry, buddy."

Anxious barked louder, then began scrabbling at the carpet, so I went over and noted almost imperceptible dents, almost as though...

"The filing cabinet's been moved, and recently!"

Chapter 6

Anxious had a second biscuit for being way smarter than me, then I shifted the cabinet to the side and got onto all fours to inspect the carpet. It was cut into a square slightly smaller than the cabinet's footprint, so I reached out to prize it up then paused, suddenly aware I was doing precisely what I had been told not to.

I glanced around guiltily, convinced the DIs would storm in and give me a right telling off, then figured it wouldn't hurt to take a peek as I could just tell them about it later and suffer the consequences. Plus, it rankled that I was finding things out that they should have discovered. The carpet came up easily enough, revealing the concrete floor beneath. No underlay? This really was a very cheap carpet install. The concrete had been hacked away in a rough square going down past the substrate to bare earth and then lined with a piece of plastic with a scrap of foam on top.

But there was nothing inside. Not a thing. Either this was old and hadn't been used for ages, or this was a secret stash hole and Simon, or someone else, had emptied it then put the filing cabinet back in place but not aligned it perfectly.

I replaced everything, moved the cabinet back to the the exact position I'd found it, then stepped back and wondered what I should do. Call Julia and let her shout at me? Keep quiet as there was nothing to see? They needed to know, so rather than get myself into bother, I called the local police station and said I had an important message for DIs Bennet and Anderson, and that they should check under the filing cabinet in the factory. I hung up before I got asked again who I was.

Duty done, I felt quite smug, and I wasn't in trouble either.

We were finished here, so I called for Anxious and we hurried through the factory and out into the bright morning.

"The freezer! I forgot to look."

With an about turn, I dashed back into the building then opened the heavy door to the walk-in freezer only to find more chaos and not the icy temperatures I'd been expecting. The walls were lined with metal storage racks containing large tubs of ice-cream like those in the shop where it was sold, but now it was nothing but liquid. Many had been torn from the shelves and created a massive mess on the floor, but there were no footprints so nobody had entered once the damage had been caused. I guessed the police believed there was nothing to see.

There wasn't. Just row after row of gone-off produce and a sickly sweet, almost overpowering smell. Anxious was in doggie heaven and I had to drag him away from what he'd decided was a free early lunch, his tongue still licking the air as I hauled him up before he got a tummy ache.

The thermostat was set to a high enough temperature to ensure nothing would remain frozen, so I could only assume that whoever had ransacked the space wanted to be certain nothing emerged from the factory intact.

Someone really hated ice-cream!

Back out in the sun, I leaned against the low wall that bisected the factories and let my body warm through. It wasn't even ten in the morning and already it was becoming uncomfortable, but I loved this weather and prayed it would last the whole summer long. Lazy days, warm nights, watching the stars, trying not to get my feet chopped off. What a summer lay ahead.

"This is nuts. What am I doing?"

I had the bug, that was for sure. I had a severe case of Amateur Detective Syndrome and knew I was in the full throes of an infection. I'd have to work my way through this if I wanted to recover, but it wasn't without serious risk.

But boy, was it exciting!

"Who are you?"

I looked up to find three women with their arms crossed staring down at me with impressive frowns on their faces. The one who spoke was in her sixties with a shock of dyed black hair, thick eyeliner, multiple rings in her ears, and one in her nose. She wore all black, consisting of tight jeans and a vest showing off an impressive figure whatever her age. The two younger women, ranging between early and late thirties if I had to hazard a guess, were like clones of the older woman. Just with less jewellery in their faces. All were trim, pretty, tanned, and ready to give me a good beating, judging by the way they were kicking at the ground with heavy biker boots.

"I'm Max. Sorry, that doesn't tell you much. I, er, I found the body of Simon on the beach, and his, er... his foot?" I don't know why I made it sound like a question, but I suppose I was feeling rather nervous and uncomfortable. Unsure what to say as I didn't know the relationship they had with Simon.

"Oh, right. Of course," said the mother, for I was certain the other women were her daughters judging by the resemblance. "Sorry to be so angry, love, but we don't want no snoopers." Her voice was a joy to listen to. A broad Welsh accent almost poetic despite the words used, and I expected English was her second language as she was clearly born and bred in these parts.

"He's the one who helped drag poor Simon from the water," said one of the daughters.

"Saved the day he did, Mum," agreed the other.

"Come and have a cup of tea, my love. You look like you need it."

"Oh, wow, a cuppa would be great. Um, who are you?"

"We work here. Or did," said the mother. "I'm Crystal, this is Ruby, and that's Amber."

"You like precious stones, I take it?"

"How did you guess?" she laughed, a gravelly tone signifying she was a heavy smoker. "My Mum's into all that new age stuff and I guess I caught the bug so picked names for my girls with deep meaning."

"They are lovely names. This is Anxious," I said, patting his head as he waited patiently for his introduction.

"Aw, isn't he sweet, Ruby?" said Amber as she bent and slapped her thighs to call Anxious over.

"Why's he called Anxious?" asked Amber, bending to play with Anxious, too, who was in his element and soaking up the adoration.

"Long story, but let's just say he isn't."

"He isn't a long story?" asked Amber, head shooting up. "Why would he be?"

"No, he isn't Anxious, you numpty," sighed Ruby.

"The man said he was."

"Enough, girls, no bickering. Let's get Max here a cuppa and he can explain why he's snooping." Crystal glared at me, arms crossed again, but then she smiled and added, "Just messing with you, love. Come on."

She marched into the factory and I knew I dared not disobey. This was a woman used to people doing as she said, and as the girls scuttled after her, I followed, wondering what insights they might have into this.

I watched from the doorway to the break room as Crystal gave the orders and the two girls jumped into action. I wasn't sure why I thought of them as girls, as they were about my age, but I suppose they acted like youngsters as they never once thought of answering back or disobeying Crystal's curt orders, and sorted out making tea in short order.

"Take a seat," said Crystal, nodding to a chair.

I dutifully sat and the sisters joined us. Crystal turned her attention to me, face friendly but with an underlying hardness that signified she'd had a tough life and wasn't about to let it slide now things were better.

"Thanks for the tea. So, you all work here?"

"We live in town, not far from here, and this job has been a lifesaver for us. Simon is... was, a great boss. Really relaxed, a chilled guy, and he paid us proper wages."

"He was a real pussycat," drawled Ruby, beaming.

"The best," agreed Amber. "But now he's dead." She hung her head, her raven hair hanging into her tea, and began to cry.

"It's alright, Sis, they'll find who did it. I bet it was that bugger who was around the other day wanting to put the rent up for the factory. Daylight robbery, it is. Poor Simon couldn't get a break."

"Don't be daft, child," chastised Crystal. "People don't kill because they want to charge more rent."

"Who do you think it could have been then?" I asked, trying to sound nonchalant as I sipped my tea.

Crystal stared at me hard until I got uncomfortable, then asked, "What's it to you? You're not from around here, and by all accounts a bit of a posh townie—"

"I am not!"

"—so why are you so interested? Snooping around here at all hours, asking questions. What are you up to, eh? What's your game, Max?"

"No game. I was just interested after I found him. I know the detectives looking into this, and thought... Okay, cards on the table?"

"It's always the best way."

"It's been bugging me. I got involved in another murder, two in fact, last week, and now here's another one. I helped last time, and I couldn't stop myself from thinking about this. I think I've got a problem, but I'm convinced the universe is telling me something. That ever since I decided to live in my campervan, this is the role I'm meant to have. Does that make sense? I feel like a total wally saying it, but it's the truth."

"You're not a wally. At least, not for the reasons you think," said Crystal, taking my hand. "There are strange forces at work in the universe, Max, and we each have our own destiny to fulfil. This might be yours. Gosh, listen to me! I sound like a right hippy," laughed Crystal, releasing my hand.

"Mum, you are a right old hippy," chuckled Ruby. "You're into all that stuff. Karma and healing and reiki and cosmic revelations."

"Only if it's true," muttered Crystal. "Max, if you believe being a nosy sod is your destiny, then you should pursue it. Be as sodding nosy as you can possibly be. Plus, if I'm reading you right, you're quite an obsessive. Single-minded, yes?"

"Very," I agreed. "Once I get into something, I lose myself to it. I focus on one thing and won't let go until it's perfect. Loose ends like this bug me no end. I can't help it. It's the way I'm wired. I've mellowed, and realise who I am, but when it comes to a man being killed, I guess I believe it deserves as much attention as possible. Not just the police, but anyone who can help."

"Well said!" called Crystal to murmurs of agreement from the sisters.

"We like him," said Amber.

"We do," agreed Ruby.

"So, what have you discovered?" asked Amber.

The three women leaned forward, dark eyes gleaming, waiting for an answer.

"Before I answer that, can I ask you all a question?" They nodded. "Was Simon an honest guy?"

When they'd finished laughing and drying their eyes, Crystal smiled sympathetically and said, "Honey, you aren't from around here so don't know the people or the customs. Everyone's as bent as a dog's hind leg. Simon more so than most. He was a character. A player, I think the youngsters call it."

"We do not!" said Amber. "We call guys like him gangsters."

"He was a gangster?" I asked.

"No, that's just what we call anyone who's a bit dodgy. But he did know gangsters, and dealt with a few."

"Yes, he was very dodgy," agreed Crystal. "Harmless stuff for the most part. A bit of ducking and diving, getting his sticky fingers into things. But sometimes he went too far, and I'm guessing this was one of those times."

"Like what? I'm not going to tell anyone, and it's just so I know more about him to help figure this out. Did he deal drugs?"

"He was into selling small amounts of dope," admitted Crystal.

"Small amounts!?" gasped Ruby. "Mum, we all know the ice-cream shop was as much a front for him selling weed as it was for keeping the tourists happy. He made a fortune."

"Don't be silly, child. It was low-level and you know it. He dabbled, that's all. A few extra quid to boost the earnings. Max, it wasn't a big deal. Simon did whatever he could to earn money, but he never hurt anyone in his life. He was a real sweetie. He treated us well, was relaxed, and a nice man. He certainly didn't deserve what happened."

"Was it gross?" asked Amber.

"Very. I found his foot in the sand, and it was shaped around him like kids had been burying someone for fun. I thought it was a dad waiting for his children to return at first, then it toppled over."

"So nasty," squealed Ruby.

"Now we've told you what you wanted, it's time for you to come clean, Max," said Crystal.

"It's not much, but I checked around in here and only found one weird thing. Is the filing cabinet usually empty?"

"No way! It's usually rammed with paperwork. He wasn't big on it, but I helped out when he got too overwhelmed."

"It's empty now, and that's not all." I explained about the hole in the floor and they insisted we go take a look.

After I'd shown them, I asked the obvious question. "Why would this be here? And who would take the paperwork?"

"I bet it's that snake from down the road," growled Amber.

"Steady, love, you can't go accusing people," warned Crystal. "But he's always had it in for poor Simon."

"Who's this?" I asked.

"Bloke who runs the competing ice-cream shop. Him and Simon go way back and have always been in competition. They started about the same time, but everyone prefers Made by Mavis rather than his rubbish ice-cream. His place is called Lovely Stuff, but it isn't. He can't ever get the taste right, and I bet he did this out of spite."

"Now who's accusing people?" said Amber smugly.

"You're right, love, I shouldn't do it. But he's such a grumpy old sod, and just plain mean. But I'm just venting, Max. We don't really think he'd do something like this. It's beyond belief is what it is."

"Any ideas what might have been hidden in the hole? Oh, and I better warn you, I called it in to the detectives, so I expect they'll be along soon. I didn't mention my name though. Probably a bit late now we're all here, but please don't bring me into it."

"We'll say we noticed the cabinet had been moved, and we saw you passing and wanted a chat," offered Crystal, all smiles.

"You'd do that for me?"

"Sure, you're now our go-to guy for solving this, so don't mess it up."

"Hey, I'm just snooping. The detectives will find who did this."

"Did someone mention detectives?" hissed Julia as she entered the break room, her solid form seeming to grow larger to fill the space, her annoyance evident. Malc squeezed past her and frowned. "You again. I should have known."

"He was just passing," said Crystal. "We dragged him in to ask about Simon. But we found something. A hole under the filing cabinet. Wanna see? And why didn't you find it?" she asked, glaring.

Crystal left to deal with them, so I waited with the sisters while they inspected the hole and asked Crystal a few questions.

When everyone returned, Julia said, "It's obvious it was you who called this in, Max, and I warned you. Stop interfering, and stop lying, or I'll have you arrested. Are we clear?"

"Yes. Sorry."

"Calls are recorded, Max, so that was a total noob mistake. Don't lie, and don't snoop. You've seen this place, so you know whoever did it means business. Simon was into all sorts and we still have a long list of people to interview, so don't get in our way."

"I understand. It won't happen again."

"It better not," warned Malc, scowling at us. "That goes for all of you. No interfering. I know Simon was good to you, at least that's what we hear, and what you said yesterday when we questioned you, but it's time to leave this to the professionals."

Once they'd left, I asked the others, "You were questioned?"

"They've been talking to everyone," said Crystal. "We couldn't tell them anything, but they came to see us yesterday afternoon. Told us not to come to work today as it was wrecked, but we came anyway. We were told we could clean up now they've finished here, so we'll do that and see what the future brings. We found this mess yesterday when we arrived, and it was just weird. Simon always came in a few hours before us to get things going, and I guess he did yesterday. But then something must have happened and he either left, or was killed here."

"Who gets this place now he's gone?"

"His partner, Lucy. She's lovely, but a bit of a wallflower. Not like Simon was. But hopefully she'll be around to sort out getting things repaired so we can carry on. We owe Simon that much."

"Sorry about your jobs, but I hope you're right and things get fixed soon. And thanks for your help."

"No problem, Max. Don't forget, we're relying on you."

I smiled at the three pairs of hopeful eyes then left with Anxious, my head full of information, but with no real idea what to do now or even if I should do anything.

Chapter 7

The morning was half gone now, but I felt like it was already late in the day. We trailed back along the road, the tourists arriving in their droves for what promised to be another perfect day. Back at Sanctuary, I opened up Vee to let some air in then slumped in my chair, feeling ready for a nap.

So I had one, grinning as I drifted off, wondering when I'd get used to this life and the fact I could doze in the morning if I wanted to.

After half an hour of restless sleep, I couldn't stand it any longer and had to move into the shade.

"Should have done that to start with," I grumbled as I dropped my chair under the sun shelter and relaxed again.

With a nice view of the tourists and the beach, I sat and watched them arrive, lugging chairs and blankets, balls and cool boxes across the road and onto the sand where they hopped about in bare feet because it was so blisteringly hot already.

At lunchtime, I had a simple bowl of cold leftovers and enjoyed every last morsel of it, much to Anxious' chagrin. But he was meant to only have two meals a day, and I'd been lax with feeding him too much so he would have to get used to it. It wasn't good for him, and although he didn't see it that way, I had decided to be stricter or he'd be a Terrier by name only, certainly not by actions.

Mickey and Sue, the couple who'd helped out confronting the culprits from the last mystery I'd found myself involved in, came down and we had a nice chat. I steered the conversation away from anything too gruesome after answering a few questions, and they seemed happy to talk about nicer things too.

It was good to see them again, and we agreed we'd get together soon for a meal, but I wasn't sure what my plans were for the day so said I'd get back to them another time. They were busy with work anyway, so didn't stay too long, reminding me that this vanlife wasn't all morning naps and extended walks. For many, it was just somewhere to live, but the nine-to-five grind wasn't a thing of the past.

After freshening up at the "bathroom," I bumped into Trev who was on his break, and I told him about the morning I'd had. He didn't want me to get involved with the Griffiths, the surname of the women at the factory. Apparently, they were well-known "characters" in the area, just like Simon had been, and most likely knew all the business he was involved in and would definitely be part of it. When I explained that they told me Simon was into marijuana selling, he laughed, explaining that half the country was to some extent as it was overtaking alcohol as the relaxation method of choice.

He also went on to say that if the Griffiths offered that information freely, Simon was undoubtedly into a lot more, but he didn't know what as he didn't get involved in anything that would risk his way of life. Smart lad.

"What made this ice-cream so great then?" I mused, half to myself.

"Everyone knows there's a secret recipe only Simon and his mum knew. Top secret stuff. I don't know if that's true, and the Griffiths have never said as much, but maybe there is. But I can tell you one thing."

"Yes?" I asked eagerly.

"Everyone around here says it's the milk."

"The milk? But milk's just milk. Okay, you can get different cream quantities, and I assume they use a lot of cream, too, but trust me, there isn't that much difference."

"That's what they say. The farm that supplies Simon is only a few miles away, and the old guy that runs it refuses to sell to anyone else. He had an agreement with Mavis decades ago and stuck to it after she passed and Simon took over. Lovely Stuff has been trying to get his milk for ages, apparently, but he sells to Simon and Simon only."

"Sold," I corrected.

"Yes, sold. Although I'm sure he'll sell to his girlfriend, Lucy. Same business."

"I guess. Okay, thanks for that. No more bodies on the beach?"

"No," he shuddered. "It was a perfect quiet morning with nothing happening at all. After yesterday, I appreciated that for the first time."

We said our goodbyes and I returned to the campervan, stopping when I spied a familiar face. This time, I knew I wasn't seeing things.

I wandered over to Volvo Barry and watched for a while as he fumbled inexpertly with his tent, seemingly no better than last time. Yet again, he put the poles in the wrong place and cursed when the tent failed to go up.

"You need to check the colours of the tags on the tent and match them with the colour of the end pole for each section," I said helpfully.

Barry turned and let the whole thing collapse, then nodded. "Thanks. Thought it was your van I spotted earlier. Have you been here long?"

"Just arrived. Did you go anywhere else after the last place?"

"Here and there. Slowly working my way along the coast."

"So you aren't following me? I thought I saw you watching me yesterday. Am I nuts?"

"You must be, as why would I do that?" Barry frowned, but his fingers kept twitching and he couldn't hold my gaze. He was a nervy guy, though, so maybe I was reading too much into the fact he kept popping up.

"Sorry, but you have to admit when you showed up without a tent it was suspicious."

"As I said, it was just a spur-of-the-moment thing. But I'm better organised now and thought I'd take time off work and enjoy the weather. But relax, I'm not a stalker," he chuckled.

"No, of course not. Nice seeing you again."

With a nod, I left him to set up camp.

The strangest thing of all was that Anxious hadn't so much as gone in for a sniff, and normally when he recognised someone he was beyond keen.

Back at the camper, I decided to take a little trip up to the farm. I was intrigued by the milk, and what made it so special. In all my years as a chef working in numerous restaurants, I'd truly never come across milk that was much different than any other. You could certainly get quality organic milk, but it was insanely expensive in comparison and not exactly common in most places.

Some of the rare breeds produced creamier milk, which was highly sought after, so maybe that was it. My chef side took over, and this was definitely something I had to check out for myself. With the directions Trev had supplied, I drove out of town and past the sand and pebble beaches of Abergele before heading off into the hills. The roads were quiet, but the ancient van struggled as usual with the incline and the twisty lanes, and once we hit a proper farm track I feared we'd never make it at all.

But the old girl was a fighter, and with me getting accustomed to the idiosyncrasies of the gearstick I managed to keep her going and followed the signs for what was apparently a very well-run farm judging by how neat the hedges were, how well-maintained the fencing was, and how happy the cows in the fields seemed.

I parked the other side of a battered metal gate and Anxious and I walked through into a vast yard with one unmistakable, overpowering smell. Cows, and what came out of their bums. I'd been to enough farms over the years to know this was usual. The yards got covered and would be washed down regularly, but not daily, meaning they would always be rather treacherous to navigate. Many farms kept cattle in vast barns year round, but it wasn't unusual for them to be out in the fields and brought in twice, sometimes three times a day, for milking in the parlours.

With the barns half empty, I assumed that this was a traditional place where they gave the animals the freedom of the Welsh countryside and all the green goodness they could eat. It was cheaper than buying in feed, but much more time-consuming. Those in the barn were presumably there to be milked, or needed extra care.

I knocked on the door of a long, stone farmhouse, the paintwork fresh, the roof recently re-tiled, and took a moment to admire the small front garden full of flowers. When nobody answered, I decided to head to the milking parlour, as maybe the owner was there.

Dogs barked from up ahead then came racing over, causing Anxious to dart forward to protect me if it came to that. I spoke softly and bent so they could see I was no threat, and the two sweet Border Collies mellowed then approached for a sniff, cautious but not aggressive. Anxious, sensing there was no fight to be had, decided he wanted to play, and next thing I knew the three of them were racing around the yard having the time of their lives. Smiling, I sauntered over to the tin-clad barn with endless milk urns outside and a sparkling truck with the farm's name emblazoned along the side. I assumed this was what delivered the milk to the factory, although how much milk could they possibly have on a daily or weekly basis? I supposed the rest was sold on somewhere, maybe to a faceless conglomerate that supplied supermarkets? Had there been a delivery the morning Simon died?

The door to the milking parlour was closed, a huge metal thing with more dents and brown stains than a prison toilet. Next to it was the barn where the cows would be herded then let into the milking zone, and the noise coming from it was incredible. The cows inside seemed anxious and jittery, their heads swaying from side to side, and they bumped into each other repeatedly. Maybe they were keen to be milked?

A smaller door within the large one gave me access, so I slid in and shut it behind me, the light blinding.

What I saw was beyond chaotic, and I couldn't process it immediately. Cows were everywhere, milk had pooled in lakes of white and brown over the filthy floor, and several pieces of machinery were damaged. The central area was sunk down with a long raised platform for the cows to stand so the apparatus could be attached easily, but something had gone horribly wrong.

Cows were now both on the platform in the the area for the workers, and were very agitated. Thick tubes that split into smaller ones—looking like something lifted directly from The Matrix—that clamped onto udders lay on the ground like dead pythons, machines hummed angrily, gigantic vats of milk, only partially full, lined up on the side wall, but none of this was as shocking as what I saw in the middle of the concrete floor.

A man wearing a traditional blue farm boiler suit and Wellington boots lay at an impossible angle on the ground, his leg strangely bent, arms a terrible mess, and that wasn't the worst of it.

I looked away, unable to stand it a moment longer as the cows trampled over everything and I began to truly fear for my own safety as they raced around the shed in a panic. Anxious yipped from the other side of the door, full of consternation. I didn't need telling twice, so sped back out, slammed it shut, and leaned back against the cool metal, trying to get my breath back.

My eyes darted this way and that, looking for someone to help, even though I knew there was no chance of saving the man inside. He'd most likely been dead for hours.

I raced across the yard towards the far end where there were several more barns and outbuildings, and searched frantically, finding nobody. But the dogs knew what they were doing and began barking at a large metal-clad building where music blared out Radio 2, so I yanked open the door, hoping for zero cows, to find I was in a workshop. A man was bent over a huge bench piled with various tools, spraying oil on a rusty bolt, the music so loud he didn't hear me shout.

I tapped him on the shoulder and he spun, eyes wide, and I raised my hands so he knew I wasn't up to anything.

"Turn it down!" I screamed, amazed he could focus with the radio so loud.

He nodded, then turned off the music on a beast of an old radio that was as battered as everything else in the workshop.

"Who are you?" he grumbled, taking a step back and eyeing up the tools on the cluttered workbench like he might need to grab a hammer or wrench to defend himself.

"I'm Max, but that's not important right now. Do you live here?"

"Live?" He seemed confused by the question, and rubbed at a short beard, his tanned face crinkling as his brow furrowed. "No, I'm not family. I work here. The boss, the old duffer, is alone now, but I do whatever he can't. Look, what's the deal?"

"You need to come with me. It's urgent, and important. He's dead. In the milking parlour. The cows have gone wild."

Anxious raced in, panting and excited, and sniffed at the surprisingly clean concrete floor before licking it. He followed the trail then pawed at an old-fashioned metal lunchbox set beside the bench. Guess he'd built up an appetite from all the playing.

"Is he yours?"

"Yes. Sorry about that. Not now, Anxious. Maybe go outside and play?" I suggested.

He glanced mournfully at the lunchbox, tapped it once just in case, whined, then dashed back out to the joyous barks of the Collies.

"Please, hurry. Someone's dead."

"What the hell are you talking about?" growled the farmhand, but I didn't wait to explain any more and ran out of the workshop.

He called after me, but I kept going and didn't stop until I was outside the shed. It was getting worse in there. The cows mooed as if in real distress, and were running around, clattering into the walls and door. I dreaded to think what the poor farmer was like now.

"Is this a sick joke?" asked the farmhand, coming to a halt beside me, face flushed and angry.

"No, I swear it isn't. The man inside is dead. What's his name, and what's yours?"

"I'm Jeff, he's Brian. And he's dead?"

"Anyone else work here?"

"No, just us."

"Then Brian's dead. And can't you hear the animals?"

We listened for a moment, then he nodded. Our eyes locked, and I shook my head to say I was sorry, but he still didn't believe me and yanked the door open and rushed inside.

Anxious darted between my legs and followed him.

I shouted, "No!" but Anxious was gone, so I had no choice but to enter too.

Neither had got far from the door as it was just too dangerous. The cows were crazed because they were clearly confused, and the one thing I knew was that they liked their routine and would be placid if things were as they should have been.

"What do we do?"

"You do nothing. Stay here, and keep the dog away. I'll sort them." He glanced at Brian, shaking his head and tutting, then eased along the way until he was up on the raised section. Jeff spoke softly to the cows as he opened a convoluted gate of sorts and the cows began to rush through.

The whole operation looked beyond dangerous, and I wasn't paying much attention to what he did or how he did it because my eyes kept returning to poor Brian.

Anxious whined, so I bent to soothe him then opened the door and we both exited, breathing deeply of the relatively fresh air comparable to inside.

I called Julia and explained where I was and what had happened, and she didn't even tell me off, just ordered me to not touch anything and stay where I was.

There was nothing I could touch that would make any difference; the whole scene was awash with cow muck, urine, milk, and blood.

Jeff emerged several minutes later and led me around to the side without saying a word, then instructed me to open and close gates to corral the animals while he goaded them into the main barn. They soon settled and happily munched on hay piled against the railings.

We went back into the yard once he was satisfied and sat on a wall, watching the dogs play.

"How could this happen?" I asked.

"He's been milking cows since a young lad. Fifty years or more. I don't know what could have gone wrong. You get a kick now and then, and they can be feisty, but never on purpose. Everyone gets dinged, and you hear about people getting trampled, but not in the milking parlour." Jeff brushed muck from his boiler suit with a thick, oil-stained hand, his eyes fixed on mine.

"Maybe a gate wasn't closed, or one got loose another way, and Brian lost control of them."

"You saw it in there. They were everywhere. That doesn't happen. Ever."

"Think it could be related to what happened to Simon yesterday? Did you hear about that?"

"Aye, terrible business. Simon was a bit of an idiot, but a good guy. He was the only one Brian would sell his milk to for ice-cream. Some long-standing contract that went back decades apparently."

"Could it be connected?"

Jeff removed his cap and scratched at greasy short brown hair, then replaced it. "I don't see how, or why. We just sold him milk. Most goes to the supermarkets where they rob us blind, so it's only selling to Simon that made it worthwhile as he paid premium prices for the best cream and milk."

"Is it really the best milk around?"

"It really is," he gushed. "It's the cows. They're special. Been bred here for generations to give relatively low yields, but it's beyond creamy and there's just something different about it. Maybe it's the special grass mix we cultivate, or how well they're looked after, but it genuinely is the best."

"And you work here every day? You didn't hear anything?"

"I've been working for Brian since I left school. He's like a father to me. Was like a father. I heard nothing. I had the radio on. We milked the girls this morning, but some need doing three times a day, so Brian always does the afternoon and I do the evening with him. Must have been in there for a few hours now. Poor bugger. What a way to go."

"I'm really sorry for your loss. It's a horrible thing to have seen."

"Not as horrible as it was for Brian. But he always said, when his time was up, he wanted to be with his animals, so he got his wish. This shouldn't have happened. It can't happen. There are all kinds of safety procedures in place to ensure they don't run riot. Something's not right."

Jeff shoved off from the wall with a determined look in his eyes and ran over to the shed and went inside.

I chased after him, knowing it wasn't the best thing for him to see Brian in such a state, and to warn him not to touch anything that the police might want to inspect.

Closing the door to ensure the dogs didn't enter, I found him staring at the body.

"Best not to look. Come on, let's go outside."

"No, not yet. I need to check things now the cows are in the shed." Jeff went through a heavy duty gate, and another, then began checking things over and grunting. He moved the sets of milking pumps, or whatever they were called, out of his way and tutted at the mess and damage, but when he got to the other side he paused, double-checked a gate, and hissed.

"What's wrong?" I called out, my voice echoing in the now quiet shed.

"Someone's left this open. Or someone opened it on purpose. Brian's been doing this his whole life and knows what to do. He double checks everything and he never makes a mistake. He knows it's too risky. This milk is valuable and he won't risk spilling a drop, so everything is meticulous. I know it doesn't look it now, but this place is kept spotless. It's almost clean enough to eat off the floor." Jeff gasped as he bent to check the gate, then his head shot up and there was genuine fear in his eyes. "Someone's removed part of the catch. It couldn't stay closed without it."

We both looked at the floor and shuddered.

"What are you saying?"

"I'm saying this was sabotage. Someone must have clobbered Brian then let the girls loose. They would panic, as they have their routine and are always so good. But they don't like change, and they get real antsy and grumpy if they can't get milked on time. It's uncomfortable for them. It hurts. They have to be milked. Here, help me with this."

"What are you doing? We can't do that. The police are coming. They need to look at everything."

"I am not going to stand around waiting for them to arrive and letting the girls suffer. Can't you hear them complaining? They need to be milked. Their udders get too full and it's dangerous. Grab that and put it there." Jeff tied the gate closed with twine from his pocket, despite my protestations.

For the next thirty minutes, after donning overalls and boots, I helped Jeff hook up hoses, opened gates, made noises at cows, and tried not to get pooed on in the face as I did something I never thought I would do in my life and milked more cows than I remembered to count. It was fast and painless for them, but I still felt like a mad scientist in a laboratory when strange suction tubes hooked on to udders with a sinister hiss and milk flowed into the vats. It was beyond surreal.

We stripped out of wellies, plastic overalls, and gloves then went outside, sweating but pleased the cows wouldn't suffer.

"Thanks. I know you didn't have to help. Pretty gross, right? All that poo and pee?"

"A bit, but I'm happy to lend a hand. But you can explain to the detectives. Julia is one formidable lady, and you don't want to mess with her."

"That's alright, I can handle her."

"You can?"

"Been doing it for years."

"So you know her?"

"Sure I do," grinned Jeff. "She's my godmother. Julia's a sweetheart when she isn't working, but yeah, she's tough when she needs to be. Let me handle her, and don't say a word about how old you think she is. I bet you thought early forties, right?"

"Something like that. I'm not good at guessing ages."

"Well, I'm forty-one, so I'll let you do the math," he chuckled. "What a day. Poor Brian. Julia will have a fit over this. She liked him."

We turned at the sound of a car, and Jeff went to open the gate for his godmother, DI Julia Bennet.

Chapter 8

They parked the car out of the way to allow the other teams space when they arrived, so I remained where I was while Jeff spoke to Julia and Malc. When they glanced my way, neither looked happy, but there wasn't much I could do about that.

Jeff tried to placate them, but it was clear it wasn't working as well as he'd hoped, but Julia still held her godson in a tight embrace and was clearly asking if he was okay, then it was all business as the detectives stormed over with Jeff trailing behind.

"We meet yet again," snapped Julia.

"Look, DI Julia, it's..."

Malc got right up in my face and said, "It's DI Bennet, and I'm DI Anderson, you got it?"

"Um, yeah, sure," I said, nonplussed.

"We aren't your friends, we aren't on first name terms, and you will show respect for our office. What did we tell you?" Malc held up a hand and said, "No, don't answer. If I recall correctly, we told you not to interfere, to stay away, to stop poking your nose in, but here you are, doing the exact opposite, and now there's another death."

"A murder," I reminded him, turning to DI Bennet, my arms open to suggest I was frustrated.

"That's not for you to decide. You're a civilian," she said curtly, clearly frustrated with me.

"Look, I get why you're annoyed, but you can't blame me for asking around and trying to help people out. Everyone's worried and scared, and I promise I'd stopped. I just wanted to come up here and see what the fuss was about with the milk. Everyone raves about it and I wanted to know why."

"It's the bloody grass they eat!" bellowed Malc, losing his cool.

"Easy there, Malc," soothed Julia, her voice softening even as she cast daggers at me.

"Julia, this wasn't anything to do with Max here," said Jeff as he joined us. "He just happened to come at the wrong time. Or make that right time. It would have been a whole lot worse inside if he hadn't arrived when he did. I know you were stopping by later on, but by then it would have been... I don't even want to think about it."

"That's not the point, Jeff. He was told not to interfere."

"Can we focus on the murder?" asked Jeff.

"Nobody knows it was murder," said Julia, sighing. "We're the ones who decide that. Don't you remember that only a few months back Brian was hospitalised because he got sideswiped by a cow in the milking parlour? He'd forgotten to shut a gate."

"That was different," protested Jeff, eyes darting to me then back to his godmother.

"You said he was always really careful and he never had an accident," I said, wondering why he'd lied.

"That was an oversight. He always checks everything properly. I've worked here for decades and he's always been strict about the protocols we have for the cows."

"Yet he still forgot," Julia reminded him. "We'll take a look, but stop with the conspiracies. This might have nothing to do with Simon's death. We know what he was like, the kind of people he was involved with. Brian was a hard-working farmer who didn't bother anyone. Who would want to kill him?"

"Someone who wanted the milk now Simon was out of the picture?" I suggested.

All three spun to me.

"Don't be ridiculous!" screeched Julia, clearly exasperated with me. "People don't murder farmers if they refuse to sell them milk! People don't have turf wars over ice-cream and bump off the opposition. You're getting carried away, Max. Just because you helped in one crime and lucked out, it doesn't mean you can make up wild stories and accuse people. You think we haven't followed up on this, spoken to people? We know our job, we do our job. But this is one hundred percent not your job. Got it?"

"I've got it," I mumbled, feeling well and truly chastised and rather ridiculous.

She was right. I had got carried away. Thinking it was most likely the other ice-cream guy, who I hadn't even spoken to yet, or the gangsters Simon dealt with. Nobody would kill a farmer to get his milk. It was nonsense. I was being a fool.

With a curt nod to me, the detectives and Jeff entered the milking parlour.

Anxious and the dogs were still playing, so I left them to enjoy themselves while I waited on the wall, unsure what I was meant to do. I got where the detectives were coming from to some extent, but was put out that they were overlooking the fact I'd discovered the hole beneath the filing cabinet, and had found the poor farmer here. How much longer would he have been in there if I hadn't arrived?

And I truly wasn't getting in their way, was I? Maybe I was. Currently, my head was all over the place, and I realised finding this body had shaken me more than I'd first thought.

It wasn't long before everyone emerged from the shed, Malc looking angry, Julia too, and Jeff looking very frustrated.

"What's wrong?" I asked.

"These idiots reckon it was an accident," said Jeff.

"Mind your attitude," warned Julia.

"Come on, you saw it in there. And the gate. No way Brian did that. Someone else did. Part of the catch was missing."

"It's the same thing he did last time," said Julia. "He left the gates open and nearly got killed. He was getting on and mistakes happen. The catch is most likely on the ground somewhere inside or got hosed away. You're being dramatic."

"I'm telling you, Brian wouldn't leave a gate like that. You saw it. Someone messed with it, took a section out."

"It's a room full of cows. Everything in there is dented and half smashed."

"They're good girls. They don't cause any damage."

"I'm not saying this is done with. We've had a quick preliminary, but will be here for hours yet. We'll go over everything properly, and you can bet there will be a thorough investigation with anyone we think pertinent being questioned. I liked Brian, we go way back, but he was getting on and quite forgetful. I know you work really hard here and he was difficult to get along with at times, but as I said, so far it looks like an accident. One of those things. I'm sorry about Brian, but don't look for answers that aren't there. And as for you." Julia turned to me, her eyes blazing behind her thick lashes. "I do not want to see you again. I do not want to hear about you talking to any suspects. I do not want anyone to mention your name."

"I just wanted to find out why the milk was so nice," I protested. "And you can't really believe this was an accident, surely? It's too much of a coincidence."

"It's not a coincidence if they aren't related. Farm accidents happen every day," said Malc. "But we're done here. I can hear the ambulance and most likely the rest of the team, so get lost, Max, and like Julia said, do not come up on our radar again or there will be consequences."

I took my cue and with a nod to Jeff I called for Anxious who raced over. His tongue was lolling, he was panting heavily, his fur was filthy, but he was happy and that was the main thing. Much to his disgust, I led him over to a tap and hosed him down—the one thing dairy farms had plenty of were taps and hoses—then dried him with his towel from the van.

By now the place was chock full of various teams. From constables, to paramedics, to forensics, and people from the coroner's office. Nobody was paying me any attention. Jeff came over and sighed as he leaned against the van.

"Sorry about Julia. She can get worked up with cases."

"I understand. They think I'm interfering. Maybe I am. I didn't mean to."

"I get it, Max. You're one of those people who doesn't like to leave things unfinished. I'm the same. I'll work and work until I drop. It's the way some people are wired."

"You know me too well," I laughed, feeling weary and stressed.

"But don't take it to heart. Julia and Malc are just annoyed that they didn't get here first. They're focusing on Simon's death, and this is an inconvenience to them. Now they have to spend time on this rather than him. They might think this is just a farm accident, but I don't."

"You're sure?"

"Positive. No way did he leave the gate that way. No way. Something's going on here, Max, I just don't know what."

"Neither do I," I admitted.

"But you're going to find out?"

"You heard what they said. I can't. They'll go crazy if I interfere."

"Then don't interfere," he said, winking. "Be discreet. Please, for me? I know we just met, but this is my whole world here and now Brian's gone. I loved that silly old guy even though we argued like cat and dog now and then. He was like a second father to me. Please at least think about this. See what you come up with?"

"Okay, sure. But, Jeff, they might be right. It could have been an accident."

"Maybe," he admitted. "I don't know. This is a real shock and I need time to process it. Nice to meet you, Max."

"Yeah, you too." I was about to leave, then figured I'd ask, so blurted, "Did you deliver to Simon's yesterday? How often did he get milk?"

"You are a smart guy, aren't you?" grinned Jeff. "There was no delivery yesterday. It was scheduled for today, but obviously that didn't happen. Julia and Malc already asked. They know their job, Max, so don't assume they skip important details."

"Right, of course."

Jeff trailed back into the chaos of people and I drove away, not knowing what to think.

Once back at the campsite, I chose not to think about much of anything and busied myself with making dinner. I was pleased that I'd set up the outdoor kitchen as it made life much easier, and it meant I could enjoy the gentle breeze coming in off the Irish Sea.

Tonight's one-pot wonder was to be a simple affair. A basic whole chicken simmered for an hour with chunks of carrot, onion, and celery. Once it had cooked and the stock was reduced, I'd add in rice to soak up the flavours then shred the lot, return to the heat, reduce again, before rejoicing at the depth of flavour. I was salivating just thinking about it, and it kept my mind off other things.

While it cooked, I settled in my chair with a still slightly funky smelling Anxious dozing fitfully beside me, and decided we would definitely have an evening stroll so he could get properly clean in the sea. Nothing like combining play and a wash without the little fella even realising.

Resigned to having no further part to play in the madness I'd maybe got too embroiled in, I relaxed into things and it came as a surprising relief. I didn't have to finish this or chase my own tail until I got the answers. This wasn't my place. It wasn't about me and I didn't have to do it. It felt nice. I was learning to let go, to stop pursuing the impossible, and accepting that not everything was down to me. I'd always had a hard time delegating, continually striving for perfection, but could let go and embrace the freedom it gave.

Then I looked up and found DI Julia Bennet looming over me, a stern look on her face, her meaty, tattooed arms crossed over her ample bosom.

"I'm not in the mood," I sighed. "I'm just sitting here waiting for my dinner to cook, okay? I'm not talking to anyone, I'm not finding any more dead bodies, although you can't blame me for that, and I'm not even thinking about the case. If you say Brian had an accident then that's fine. You know better than I do. I'm just an ex-chef who wants a quiet life."

"Max, I might not know much about you, but one thing I do know is that you are not the kind of guy that wants a quiet life. You like the adrenaline rush. You enjoy adventure. You love a challenge."

"I do like a challenge, and yes, I do love adventure. I always thought I became a chef because of my passion for food, but it was more than that, I think. I liked the buzz. The high of the pressure. But I went too far and now I'm close to doing it again."

"No, you aren't," she said softly. "You're a caring guy and you want to help. You aren't rushing around like a headless chicken shouting at people. You're using your brain and letting things seep into your subconscious. That's how all the best police are. You'd make a fine detective," she grinned, scratching at her arm and not making eye contact.

"You think so?" I brightened.

"Sure. A very good one. I know you said you used to be overly stressed and very single-minded, but it's obvious you're a pretty chilled guy nowadays. You don't get too worked up or dramatic, you think about things, and seem to have a very uncanny and annoying knack of being in the right place at the wrong time."

"Or the wrong place," I muttered.

"That's just semantics. What I'm trying to say is, you're a good guy. Malc and I were harsh on you because we were frustrated, understand? We don't want you stepping on our toes."

"I didn't mean to."

"I know, and to be fair, you didn't really. We're up to our necks with this thing with Simon, and working in these local places is tough for everyone. Close-knit communities are hard to police, as there are always skeletons in the closets. Some of these family feuds go back generations and nobody even knows why they started. Everyone's got an opinion, and it often isn't positive. An outsider offers a new outlook, so don't beat yourself up over it."

"I didn't mean to interfere."

"You didn't. Much. After that mess in Rhyl, and you doing your big reveal, it rankled, I admit. You beat us to it, Max, and we were left hanging. You tied clues together we didn't think of, although to be fair you didn't really share all of them, so when you turned up here and we got another body, you can understand our annoyance."

"Of course. But I just found Simon on the beach."

"I know, and that's why I came to apologise."

"You did?"

"Yes. Look, cards on the table time?"

"Sure. Let me get you a seat." I rose and put the chair out for Julia. She sank into it, frowning at the tight fit, but sighed as she kicked off her shoes and wiggled her toes.

"This is the life, eh? Watching the world go by."

"It's amazing. I'm loving it so far. It's been good for me, despite what's happened. I feel like I'm becoming the man I should have been many years ago."

"Good for you. So, what I came to say is, ignore what we said earlier. If you can find anything out, then have at it. Do it discreetly, don't act like you're an officer, don't go getting in anyone's way, but if you happen to think of something, or get any clues, then let me know."

"You're sure? This is a big change of heart."

"Yes, I know. Actually, it was Malc's idea."

"Now that I find hard to believe," I laughed.

"I know, right?" chuckled Julia. "I was shocked too. But like I said, we both think you have the nose for this. You're a natural. Your mind processes information and works things out. You have the gift. Don't let me regret this, Max. And I understand if you don't want to be involved and you pack up and leave, but if you are hanging around then keep your senses open and see what you might uncover."

"I will. And thank you, Julia. This is very kind of you."

"Hey, I'm a sweetheart underneath this gross lump of a body."

"Don't talk like that. You're a very confident woman, and I'm surprised you say that about yourself."

"Max, nobody is how they seem. You should know that. I put on this front, but I'm the same as everyone else. I wish I was thin, I wish I was pretty, I wish I had a pay rise, but life's not like that. Don't screw me over, Max, or I will destroy you, understand?"

I laughed and said, "Sure," but Julia wasn't laughing and she wasn't joking around. "Yes, I won't."

"Good. Now, enjoy your dinner, and tread lightly. Don't obsess, don't go annoying anyone, and I meant what I said about not wanting to see you. Just do your thing, but do it quietly."

Julia heaved out of the chair then left through the gate to the road.

Dinner was almost ready, so I finished off the rice then dished Anxious and myself up a glorious feast then mulled over my conversation with Julia while I savoured every last morsel. What on earth was I meant to do next?

In the end, the answer was simple.

Nothing. I'd do precisely nothing.

Chapter 9

After our delightful dinner, I focused on cleaning up and yet more organising—I was beginning to realise this was a big part of my life now. Long live the stackable clear plastic box with a lid! I had my cooking utensils in a small container, my plates and bowls in another, and perishables in yet another, all neatly piled one on top of the other. It kept things organised, clean, and right where I needed them with the added benefit that they could easily be moved in and out of the campervan.

Once that was done, and with the day cooling to a comfortable temperature, I had a workout. I'd been lax about exercise since this all began, but was determined to stick to my regime now. After spending a year getting in shape and losing a little weight, I didn't want to become a lazy slob; I wanted to look the best I ever had.

Smug as only those who've exercised when they know others around haven't, I hit the showers, suffered the cold water, then took Anxious for a walk along Abergele Beach. This whole section of coast almost met back up with Rhyl, the large holiday parks to the east not in such numbers the further along to the west you got, but I wondered for how long.

As we crossed over to the sand, a stream of large trucks arrived, along with a veritable posse of cars, caravans, and huge trailers. The fair was coming to town!

I'd have to let Min know, as she adored the fair. Should I? Maybe not.

Only a few people remained on the beach, so it was like we had the entire coast to ourselves. No need to worry about Anxious kicking sand into people's sandwiches, or getting stern looks when he had a pee on a sandcastle.

We headed straight for the water, and I used the flinger to throw the ball over and over until my mucky pup smelled fresh and was suitably tired. On our way back up the beach, a man approached. He had long wavy hair of a light brown hanging to his naked chest, wore a pair of three-quarter checkered shorts, and was barefoot. His tan was so deep he was almost black. One of those people who can seemingly just get darker and darker without reaching the end of their melanin quota.

He had a broad grin on his face, and I wondered why, but it seemed to be directed at me. Definitely the friendly type. I estimated him to be in his early forties, but that was debatable. Anxious seemed to take an instant like to him and raced ahead then jumped up at his legs for a fuss, which was given gladly and with a hearty laugh.

I stopped beside them and said, "Sorry about him. He takes to some people right away, but they don't always appreciate his affection."

"Hey, man, no problem. He's a cutie, aren't you?" The man plonked himself down on the sand carelessly, and rolled around with Anxious going crazy with excitement.

Since when did humans become so much fun? I could see him thinking as he jumped onto the guy's stomach and began licking his chin.

"You really like dogs then?" I asked, laughing along at their antics.

"Sure. Who doesn't? But I lost my best friend a few months back and I'm still grieving. She was everything to me, but you have to accept the fleeting nature of existence, you know?" he said, his piercing blue eyes never leaving mine.

"I know. It's the way of things. You have to enjoy the time you have with them."

"Absolutely, man, you get it. I'm Haitch by the way."

"Haitch?"

"As in the letter H for hotel. Full name's Harry, but it doesn't fit the vibe, so H it is. You cool with that?"

"Um, yes, I'm cool with it. I'm Max. I'm staying at Sanctuary. Got there this morning."

"Ah, the infamous Max of the 67 splittie," H beamed, lifting a hand to be hauled up.

I dutifully helped him up and he slapped me on the back and said, "Cheers. So, you enjoying your stay?"

"Yes, and I owe you money for the pitch."

"Don't sweat it. Any time. I'm around."

"Okay, that's great."

"Hear you've been having some stressful times? Bodies, feet, and you found poor Brian at the farm, yeah?"

"News travels fast around here," I frowned.

"Dude, you wouldn't believe how fast. The gossip grapevine is better than the phone signal here. People love to talk. It's a Welsh thing."

"It has been a mad few days," I admitted.

"Brian didn't deserve to go out like that, although he always said he'd rather get killed by a cow than by old age. Guess he got his wish. And as for Simon..." H's face soured at the mention, so there was obviously something going on there.

"What, not a fan?"

"He was cool and all that, but not my kinda guy. Too dodgy. He sold good weed, but he wasn't my favourite man. Bit too intense, if you know what I mean?"

"Not really, no," I admitted.

"Mixed with dangerous people, never satisfied with his lot. Guy was dumb as he had a thriving business, earned enough in the season to shut up the shop for months in the winter and cruise on the earnings. But he couldn't just be happy. He was always out for more. More money, more trouble, more everything."

"Apparently, he had a few enemies, like the other ice-cream place," I hinted.

"Yeah, but that's just friendly competition. Nothing too serious. And the owner isn't the kind of guy to murder someone, trust me."

"You know him well?"

"I know everyone. Chester's a grumpy old git, no doubt, and he hates that Simon always did better than him, but kill him? No way. I've known him a long time, my parents even longer."

"Okay, thanks for that."

"What gives with you, Max?" H frowned as he studied me, like he could read my personality. It was slightly unnerving.

"How'd you mean?"

"I mean, why'd you care? Why are you so interested?"

"I want to help. A man's dead, two men actually, and they deserve justice if there is justice needed."

"Amen, brother. That's what I wanted to hear. I like you, Max, so consider your stay free. Don't argue, it's a nominal amount anyway. My folks gave me the land a long time ago and it grew from there, but you can always find me up at the top of the field in my bus. It doesn't run anymore, but I found my home where I least suspected. Back where I grew up. Funny how things work out, eh?"

"Sure is. And thanks for the freebie. So, while we're chatting, who do you think did it?"

"Wow, you don't mess about, do you?"

"Better to be direct, right?"

"Oh yeah, and it's refreshing. Now, who could have chopped off Simon's foot then killed him? Could be anyone. Not people I know or want to know. Not Chester, he wouldn't dare, so I guess the answer is I don't know. As for Brian, everyone liked him. That might just be an oversight on his part. He was getting on, and had an accident the other month. I heard about Jeff insisting it was no accident, but he's just too close to things up there."

"Thanks, H, that's very helpful. I guess I'll see you at the campsite?"

"Sure, I'm always around. Be careful, Max, and don't push people around. They don't appreciate it, especially from outsiders. We have our own ways of doing things around here, if you get my drift?"

"It's the same everywhere, H. Everyone's got their own traditions and ways of handling things in different places. I've been around."

"I can tell. Take it easy, brother." H gave Anxious a tummy tickle as the daft dog rolled over to accommodate him, then he began whistling as he wandered along the beach.

I wondered if he was stoned, or just had that hippy vibe some people seemed to be born with. Maybe he was simply content with his lot. H was one of those rare people that actually had what they wanted out of life, or was happy with what life had given him. Maybe it wasn't perfect—whose life was?—but if he'd found peace with that then surely life truly couldn't get any better?

One day I'd listen to my own advice. Maybe.

At the top of the beach where sand met road, I sat and just let the special quiet time of day envelop me. There was something magical about the evening by the coast. A calmness, a stillness that went beyond a lack of tourists or endless cars, but a feel in the air. I made the most of it before I returned to the campsite and decided to have an early night.

Tucked up in bed with Anxious before it was truly dark outside, I felt safe and happy. With a good book, I read for a while, then turned off the light and fell asleep to the snoring of my perfectly content dog.

The morning brought several surprises. One was that it was suddenly cold, the wind was blowing a gale, and the sun had become stuck behind a queue of dark clouds lining up to make it an overcast day. Two, I'd forgotten to do any laundry since I arrived and my jeans and all my underwear bar one pair were dirty.

This came as a shock for two reasons also. One, the forecast was meant to be guaranteed sun and warm weather. Two, I had never been to a laundrette in my life.

Time to figure it out.

After a light breakfast, Anxious and I headed into town on foot as everything that needed washing fitted easily into a backpack. No point driving when I didn't have to, and Anxious needed the walk anyway. The difference in the number of people was incredible. The weather had kept tourists away, and I didn't blame them. Sand and salt tore through streets, carried on angry gusts that blew the trees and made signs for coffee shops and cafes bang noisily. Rubbish tumbled down the roads as we battled valiantly against the wind tunnelling straight at us through narrow side streets.

When we made it into a sheltered area out of the weather, the difference was astonishing, as though my hearing had resumed. I found the laundrette and pushed apprehensively through the door, then stood there, soaking in the warmth caused by the oversized washers and dryers. The smell was intense, a real combination of dirty washing, cleaning products, and that peculiar smell you only get from the dry heat caused by tumble dryers. Combine that with the dampness of the washing machines, and you had a hot and humid environment perfect for tropical plants, of which there were precisely none.

Armed with a pocketful of change, as that's what I'd been told I would need, I stepped back in time and into another world. The place was full of old ladies, students, holidaymakers, and people like me. Travellers. Those touring the country, living in campervans or motorhomes, whatever it was we were meant to be called. Vanlifers? It didn't matter. I could recognise one of what I thought of as my own now. Maybe it was the smugness we radiated. With a few knowing nods, and some friendly smiles to the old ladies, I approached a machine and read the instructions.

It seemed simple enough, so I added my detergent, closed the door, dropped in the coins, and away we went.

Only then did I realise why everyone was looking rather bored. You had to wait about an hour for the washing to be done, and it didn't seem acceptable to leave your machine and go off. You were meant to wait with it. Just to be sure, I sat next to a guy tapping on his phone and asked, "Excuse me. Do we have to wait here? How come nobody leaves and returns when the washing is done?"

"First time, eh?" he asked, nodding knowingly as he lifted his gaze.

"You can tell?"

"Always," he laughed. "You have to stay. It's the rule."

"What rule?" I looked at the list of actual rules pinned to the wall, but that was about litter and ensuring you didn't leave any clothes behind.

"The unwritten one. Nobody leaves. You have to get your stuff out the moment it's finished. It's just manners, yeah? These places get busy and what if you forgot the time or got held up somewhere? People would be waiting. That's not fair on them. So you wait, then you go when you're done."

"Fair enough," I said. "Thanks."

"No problem. Enjoy it. It's kinda zen once you get into it. Good place for a kip. Close your eyes, listen to the drums, and enjoy the heat. It's freezing out there."

"Good idea. I might do that."

I moved over to a chair where I could lean back, then told Anxious he could get onto my lap. With him curled up, I closed my eyes, listened to the whirr of the machines, the background hum of people talking in hushed tones as though in a library, and sure enough I was soon asleep.

When I stirred, the man I'd spoken to was gone. So were several others. But there were new, almost identikit people in their place, everyone obeying the unwritten law and sitting in front of their chosen machine and watching, waiting, maybe even praying.

"What do you think, Anxious? Do you like it in here?"

Anxious yawned, then closed his eyes again with a grumble. He liked it.

Right on time, the door to my machine popped open so I placed Anxious on the floor then took my sweet-smelling clothes to the dryer, but then recalled that the jeans weren't meant to be tumble dried as they'd get ruined. So I kept them out, put the rest in, and added more coins.

More waiting. This time, not as much fun. What if you had things to do? When would you fit this in? It was hard to break ties with my old way of living, reminding myself that if need be I would do my laundry on a weekend or after work the same as countless others no doubt did. Being so used to the fast pace of the modern world, this slower approach was still taking some adjusting to.

Checking around for something to occupy me, I noticed one of the Griffiths women at the end of the row of plastic seats. She was staring blankly into space, a frown on her face accentuated by the heavy, dark makeup, the black hair, and matching clothes. She seemed upset but trying to hide it, and I wasn't sure if I should go over and say hello or leave her be.

The decision was taken out of my hands because she must have sensed she was being watched so lifted her head and turned her attention my way. I smiled and said a quiet, "Hello," much to the shock of the lady sitting next to me who scowled then continued with her knitting.

Ruby smiled back, her face lighting up like she was pleased to see me, so taking that as an invite, I moved over and sat beside her.

"Everything okay?" I asked. "You seemed upset."

"Oh, I'm fine. It's just been one of those days, you know? Poor Simon, and all that damage at the factory. Us out of a job, at least for now, and Mum and Amber so stressed about the future. It's a mess is what it is."

"I'm sorry to hear that. You relied on the work, eh?" Ruby frowned at me, not understanding. "Sorry, that was dumb. Of course you relied on the work. It was your job, and everyone needs money. Sorry."

"That's okay. I know what you meant. I think. It's tough for us. There aren't many jobs around here, and definitely none where we get to be together. We've always been like this. We're a team and very close. We do everything together. But I think this is the end of that. Amber's been talking about moving away for a while to try her luck down in Cardiff. She wants to be near some action, is what she says. Cardiff's not too big, but it is a city and she really might go. While the work was stable she was happy enough to stay, but now Simon's gone I think she might do it. I can't be without my sister, I just can't. I've seen her every single day of my life. She's a little older, you see. What will I do without her?"

"Gosh, that does sound rough. You live together then?"

"Yes, of course. Just us girls. Mum's always looked out for us and we hang out all the time. It's our thing. We're like sisters really. But Amber has had itchy feet for a year or two now. Keeps talking about leaving. Now she's got the perfect excuse. If Lucy, that's Simon's partner, doesn't decide to keep running the place, then there's no work. Even if she does, it will be months before things can get sorted, so then what?"

"I'm so sorry to hear all that. But maybe the factory can open back up sooner? I suppose it depends on what Lucy decides to do. Have you spoken to her?"

Ruby shook her head sadly. "We didn't want to interfere. She's been dealing with the police, and it's such a shock to her. And, well, I shouldn't be saying this, but we never got on. She's not the friendliest of women, and she doesn't seem to like us much."

"Nobody has to like everyone, especially if they aren't friendly. I thought you were all one big happy family in the business?"

"No, we work at the factory and the shop is separate. Lucy has always been in charge there, and sometimes it made life difficult for Simon."

"How come?"

"Because he was always the go-between, getting stressed when Lucy sent him to the factory to ensure we were going to be on time with the ice-cream, that kind of thing. She sometimes even complained about it, relaying messages to us that Simon hated giving, but he did it anyway. He was such a nice guy, a bit dodgy, but nice with it. Lucy ran the shop well, I'll give her that, and it was a very good business for them both, but they had their ups and downs over the years."

"But they were close? In love? You trust her?"

Ruby's hand shot to her mouth as her eyes popped, then shook her head vehemently. "She's a pain, and certainly not a friend, but she would never hurt Simon. They were a proper team, and in love, and had been together for like ever. It's kind of sweet. Or it was. She loved him, and she's certainly not about to go and chop off his foot and leave him on the beach. What kind of woman would do something like that?"

"One who found out her partner was having an affair maybe? Or there were money troubles. I honestly don't know, but somebody did it to him."

"Not Lucy. I should pay my respects soon, but I'm not sure she'd appreciate it. Maybe it's the way we look, or that we're women, but she's never been nice to any of us. Mum says to steer well clear, but maybe I'll pop by later."

"She's in the flat above the shop?"

"Yes, it's quite a nice place, apparently. Maybe you should go," Ruby offered brightly, looking cheered at the prospect. "You can say you're sorry and pass on our best wishes."

"Maybe I should," I mused. "I did find Simon, so maybe paying my respects is the right thing to do."

The door on the dryer opened so I stood to gather my things. Once folded, I turned to smile at Ruby but her eye were glazed and she didn't notice me until I cleared my throat to get her attention.

"I'll see you around?"

"Sure, Max, and it's been nice meeting you."

"You too. I'm staying at Sanctuary now, so if you ever need someone to talk to, or think of anything about this madness, then you know where to find me."

"Thanks. Later."

I woke Anxious with a low whistle, getting a stern frown from the knitting lady, and he stumbled after me, yawning. The heat of the laundrette sure did make you sleepy, and I felt content and welcome in this strange cocoon of a place.

We emerged from its comforting embrace into yet another world entirely.

Chapter 10

Anxious howled with disgust as the door closed behind us and we were confronted with a deluge of rain that made me think of all kinds of biblical things. My already sopping Terrier pined as he scratched at the door, hoping to return to the warmth, but we had things to do, although, in fairness, none of them were pressing.

What did we have to do? Visit Lucy and possibly give her some closure? That was doubtful, as what could I say? But I should see her, I knew that, and had been putting it off. What else? Nothing really, unless I was going to poke my nose into things that weren't my business. The conversation with Julia had hit home, even though I was certain there was something I was missing and might discover if I kept asking around, but the last thing I wanted to do was hinder the investigation. This was, after all, murder, possibly two murders.

People dashed past with umbrellas or their coats over their heads as the streets became like a river. Anxious and I squished ourselves under the overhang of the laundrette and watched, astonished, as the road disappeared.

"We'll have to wait it out. No point drying clothes then getting them soaked again."

Anxious cocked his head in his familiar way, waiting for me to do something about all this water.

"Hey, it's not my fault. And what's with you anyway? If we were at a river or the beach, you'd be straight in the water, so what's the difference?"

He whined like I was a fool for not understanding, then sighed as he lay down and rested his chin on his paws.

"Give it a minute and it might stop. It's not supposed to rain, and it's not exactly freezing now, so maybe this will blow over."

Even as I spoke, the rain and clouds began to disperse. I decided it was best to make a break for it, so we sloshed along the pavement, watching the drains gurgle as the water raced into the mysterious underworld beneath our feet.

As we weaved our way through town, people began to emerge from shops and doorways, laughing and smiling at the return to typically unpredictable British weather. I looked up to find that the clouds were thinning and a hint of blue could be seen to the east as the sun burned through, so my spirits lifted as we retraced our route and headed back towards the seafront.

The humidity began to climb, and suddenly, making me sweat. Along with a crowd of other people, I stopped at a paved area and watched, amazed, as the air shimmered. The sun burst free from its grey prison with an intensity that almost blinded me as it reflected off the paving and clouds of steam enveloped everyone.

I gasped along with the rest of them, marvelling at the rising heat as the world turned almost white with the ferocious sun. It was a remarkable sight, and a reminder of the power of nature.

Within minutes, it was as though the rain had never happened. The streets shone with a fresh glory as they baked, washed clean of dirt and debris, like the whole town had been given a spring clean. People were bemused, but happier than I'd ever seen anyone in a town. Relieved that the nice weather wasn't just temporary, but that maybe the forecast had actually been genuine and not a cruel trick.

We continued on our way, Anxious skipping along merrily beside me, nodding and smiling at people as we went. Something made me pause and I turned to investigate, but saw nothing out of the ordinary. I got a distinct Volvo Barry vibe, but he was nowhere to be seen. He'd got under my skin, and I knew he was up to something.

Across the road, a shop was busier than the others, with people queueing up outside. Most likely taking advantage of the large canopy. It was the other ice-cream place, Lovely Stuff, the lettering in bright curved script across the glass front, with various signs listing the options, the *t* in the shape of a cone.

What was the owner's name? Who'd told me? Maybe Trev had mentioned it, or the Griffiths women? That was it. Chester. I'd been in there yesterday, not giving it a moment's thought, and he'd been surly, uncommunicative, and hardly seemed pleased about the extra business. And he hadn't been gossiping with customers about the death of his rival. At the time, I'd thought nothing of it, but looking back on it now it did seem rather odd. Could it have been him after all?

I decided to get myself and Anxious an ice-cream, more to get a feel for things than anything else, as you never knew what you'd hear in a queue and it might be insightful. We crossed the sparkling road and took our turn at the back of the line, but it moved rapidly and soon enough we were outside and could read the menu.

Once inside, I overheard an elderly woman talking loudly and dramatically so listened along with everyone else.

"...be after you next. What if it's a gang out to murder the local ice-cream shop owners?"

"Don't be daft," grumbled the man I recognised as Chester as he handed the woman a plain vanilla ice-cream in a basic cone and she took it with a frown.

"Is that all I get? I wanted a double."

"That is a double. I saw Mary do it. You know how they're served, same as everywhere else. One scoop pushed down into the cone, one on top. Don't go trying to cause trouble, Celia. We've all got enough on our plate."

She grumbled, then a wicked smile spread across her face as she said, "What if you're next? You should watch yourself."

"Nobody's killing shop owners," insisted Chester. "We know Simon was into all sorts, and now he's paid the price."

There were gasps from several people, presumably locals who knew the gossip, but nobody argued.

There were murmurs of drugs and gangsters and bad eggs, but everyone agreed the ice-cream was good, much to Chester's chagrin.

The old lady frowned at her purchase but left. Chester sighed in relief and spread his hands as if to say, what can you do?

Two women were busy serving customers and taking payment, so Chester took the opportunity to come from behind the counter then left through the front door. The younger woman, possibly a teenager, busied herself re-stocking the cones, so a woman in her early forties beamed at me, her slender frame and stylish, short hair reminding me of a raven because her mannerisms were so birdlike.

"What can I get you, love?" she asked, frowning as she noticed a dark smudge on her white apron. She tutted, then held up her hands and said, "Just once, I'd like to go a whole day without getting this thing filthy."

I read her name tag, Heidi, so said, "Two raspberry ripples in waffle cones, please, Heidi."

"Coming right up."

I was served promptly and, yes, with two scoops.

"You're getting a lot more custom, I see," I said, nodding my thanks to Heidi.

"It's been crazy. It was a terrible thing, but business sure is booming." She smiled, then realised she wasn't supposed to be happy about someone's death so tried to look sad. It wasn't very convincing.

"Bet you'll be running out soon," I laughed.

"Oh no, Chester was up at the crack of dawn and at his factory to ensure everything was ready. We knew we'd be buzzing today. And before you ask, just like everyone else has, he was at the factory from four the morning Simon was killed. I was there with him, so he didn't do it."

"Um, thanks." I took the ice-creams, swiped my card, then we left as the press of people in the shop increased.

We crossed the road to get some space, then moved back down a side street only to find Chester there in a small courtyard, sitting on a bench.

As we approached, he looked up then ignored us and continued tapping on his phone.

"Hi. Mind if I sit?"

"Suit yourself," he grumbled, eyes locked on the screen.

I put my laundry beside the bench, then chuckled as Anxious sat, attention fixed on the treat.

"Will you look at this guy? He'll freak out if I wait any longer before I give him his snack."

Chester glanced up, grunted, then swiped his phone.

With a shrug to Anxious, I gave him his cone and he tucked in happily, devouring half of it in two bites then licking at the fast-melting ice-cream as it pooled on the ground.

I tasted mine, surprised to find it was a little better than the day before. Not award-winning, but not bad either.

"Hey, tastes great," I said brightly, nodding to the runny raspberry ripple as it dripped down the cone. I licked it rapidly, enjoying the hit of fruit.

"It should. We have the best recipe and pride ourselves on making it ourselves."

"So you have a factory too? By Simon's?"

Chester frowned, then took notice of me for the first time. "Do I know you?"

"No, I don't think so. I'm Max. I'm the one who found Simon on the beach."

"That must have been awful," he said, voice strangely monotone, eyes sharp as he took me in.

"It was. Very strange, and very upsetting. The lifeguard, Trev, was with me, and it was even worse for him. Do you know him?"

"I know everyone around here. Born and bred."

"Right, yes."

"The tourists are keeping you busy, though, I see. Lots of extra business."

"Yes, it's been mad busy ever since they had to shut. Good for me, but it's not how I wanted it. I wasn't a fan of Simon's, but I'd never wish what happened even on my worst enemy."

"Bet the police had you down for questioning, eh?

"Why would they? We just had a chat. Are you saying I should be a suspect?" he hissed, shoulders bunching, fists balling.

"No, of course not. I don't know anything about it. I just assumed that's what they'd do. How they operate." I shrugged, not wanting to get on his wrong side.

"Yes, well, it doesn't work like that. Everyone around here knows we had a thing, but that it was just healthy rivalry. Nothing more."

"Of course not. What do you think happened then?"

"He got too deep into business he shouldn't have and ended up with his foot chopped off. Not my problem. And it isn't yours either. Why do you care?"

"I'm a caring kind of guy," I laughed, but he didn't see the funny side of it. "But in truth, it's because I found him. I want to know why someone would do that to another human being."

"Then you're asking the wrong person. Excuse me." Chester stood, then wandered back towards the shop. I watched him go, wondering if he was just a surly man or there was more to this.

I definitely needed to distance myself from this thing, and I intended to do exactly that once I'd spoken to Simon's partner. When you began to suspect shop owners of bumping off the competition and possibly the farmer who wouldn't supply you with the best milk, it was definitely time to get a new hobby.

Next I'd be suspecting the mother and daughters team. After all, didn't Ruby say that Amber had been wanting to leave for ages and now she had the perfect excuse? Maybe she did it so the factory would shut and she could leave and go it alone in Cardiff?

"I need a less gruesome interest," I told Anxious as I turned. "Hey!"

Anxious licked his lips and wagged happily. I stared at the remains of my cone and sighed. He'd eaten it down to a tiny piece while I was distracted, and he didn't look guilty in the slightest.

With my laundry over my shoulder, I led Anxious back out into the blistering sunshine, dumbfounded by the change and the fact tourists were now wandering around in bikinis and shorts when half an hour ago I was considering buying a kayak to navigate the streets.

We returned to the campsite so I could dump my laundry, then headed back out to visit Lucy, who must be distraught at the loss of her life partner.

The shop was obviously shut, with a sign in the window saying they were closed for the foreseeable future. I walked down the side street and found the door for the flat upstairs and rang the bell. Nobody answered. Maybe it was broken. Maybe she was out.

On a whim, and I don't know what possessed me, I tried the handle. The door wasn't even closed properly and it squealed open so I peeked inside and found a staircase leading up. The carpet was an expensive coir, the walls freshly painted and hung with abstract art. A small alcove held shoes, boots, and wellingtons, along with several coats, and everything smelled amazing and was immaculate.

I heard banging from upstairs and wondered if I should either leave, call out, phone the police, or snoop.

With a suspicion that Anxious had picked up on my indecision, he decided to take matters into his own hands and raced up the stairs then stopped at the top and sat, tail brushing the carpet.

Glancing back outside, I was still in two minds, then I heard a scream and shouting and Anxious disappeared, so

I took the stairs two at a time, my heart hammering in my chest. Anxious was around the corner on the landing, crouched low and sniffing at a partially opened door.

Another was at the far end of the hallway, with two more either side. I assumed one was a bathroom, one a bedroom, and the open door to a room at the end was a spotless kitchen.

A woman shouted, "Leave me alone!" so I put my back to the wall beside the open door and risked a peek, cursing my foolishness silently. Stressed, I waved at Anxious until he came beside me and sat. I put my finger to my lips and he laid down; he was such a good dog.

"We already told you, it doesn't work like that. Simon had our gear, and we want what it was worth. You owe us a great deal of money."

"And I told you, I don't know where it is. He's dead, don't you understand? Did you kill him?" gasped who I assumed was Lucy.

"We'll kill you if we don't get our stuff and the cash. It's worth a fortune and we know you were helping him pass it on. Don't try to pull a fast one on me, Lucy. You know what will happen if you do. Simon's demise is unfortunate, but let it be a lesson. Don't play with matches if you don't wanna get burned. Where is it? It's not at the factory, so where?"

"Did you damage the equipment? Was that you?" hissed Lucy, a tremble in her voice that meant she was very frightened. I wasn't doing too well either.

"This isn't twenty questions. We looked, we found nothing. So it must be here. I want what's owed. With interest."

"Get out!" screamed Lucy, and something smashed against the door.

The sounds of a scuffle were unmistakable, and I was about to call the police when Anxious barked then ran into the room, growling.

With no other option, I plastered a fake smile on my face and barged in, calling loudly, "Lucy, are you in here? Hello? I wanted to come and offer my condolences and the door was ajar." I crunched over the broken remains of a ceramic ornament, then stopped as two men wheeled from Lucy to confront me.

"Who are you?" demanded a man in his thirties in a simple black shirt, dark jeans, with a crew cut and a nasty red burn on his jaw that ran like a twisted river beneath his open shirt collar.

"A boyfriend?" sneered the other man, who was more like a teenager really, and I guessed he was. He wore a paisley tracksuit with the largest pair of white trainers I had ever seen, and a thick gold chain. He was extremely pale, which was unusual for anyone who lived by the coast.

"Sorry to barge in," I boomed, "but the dog here shot up the stairs and I heard voices so assumed you didn't hear the bell. Is it working?"

"Is what working?" asked the youth.

"The bell," I said with a frown. My eyes drifted to Lucy who looked upset and shaken but not hurt. She was, understandably, very confused by my appearance as she didn't have a clue who I was, but she looked relieved too.

"These men were just leaving," said Lucy, taking advantage of the opportunity.

"And we were having such a nice chat too," drawled the boss, raising an eyebrow in a bemused way, not at all unnerved by my presence or that of Anxious who was still growling.

"Just leave!" shouted Lucy.

"Think she means us or you?" asked the youngster. "Who are you again?"

"I don't think introductions are needed, not unless you both go first," I said, locking eyes with the boss.

"Mate, if you don't know who I am then you aren't from around here. Maybe another time?" He smiled, cold and reptilian, then turned to Lucy and warned, "This isn't over."

They nodded to each other, then brushed past me and left. Anxious ran to the door and barked a warning as they descended the stairs. The front door banged shut and only then did Lucy release a ragged breath and collapse into the nearest chair.

Like the rest of the flat, it was modern, clean, and minimal. The living room held another chair, a matching sofa, a sixties coffee table, a large TV, and more abstract art.

"Good job, Anxious," I congratulated, forgiving him for the ice-cream pilfering.

"Excuse me?" asked Lucy.

"Yes?"

"Who the hell are you, and what are you doing in my home?"

It was a fair enough question. The answer would not improve her mood.

Chapter 11

"I'm Max. I apologise for the scare. I'm not here to hurt you or cause any trouble, I promise."

"Another one who Simon owed money to, I expect," she hissed, eyes darting towards the door, foot tapping.

"No, not at all. I'm the one who found your partner on the beach. I'm so sorry, and thought it only right I should come and see you to offer my sympathy and check you were okay."

"Gosh, so sorry for being rude." Lucy sighed deeply, swatted at her hair, and smiled weakly. "Max, you are welcome. Please, take a seat. Can I offer you a drink? Excuse me for being so brusque, but in case you hadn't noticed, those men weren't exactly friends and I was terrified."

"I heard. At least some of it. How are you?"

"Holding up, but annoyed beyond belief with Simon for leaving me in this mess. How could he?"

"You didn't know about his, er, rather less that always legal sidelines?" I took the offered seat and sank back into a soft chair that smelled of lemon.

"No offence, but what do you know about it? From what I heard about you, you don't live here and hardly know anyone. You were with that lifeguard, weren't you?"

"Yes, that's Trev. We discovered your partner. Terrible, and so upsetting, I'm sure."

"It really is. Poor Simon didn't deserve that. But I'm relieved you came. I think it would have got violent here if you hadn't arrived."

"Then I'm glad I did. Is there anything I can do?"

"You can prove those horrible men killed Simon and get them put where they belong. In jail."

"Are you sure it was them?"

"Not really, no. In fact, it might not have been. It could have been someone else just as nasty."

"Did you know about Simon and his dealings with them?"

"I kept out of his other business, asked no questions, and played no part in it," she huffed, tugging a thin blue cardigan around her chest as though it could ward off the bad guys. Her brown hair was cut into a very neat bob and her features were almost elven, with high cheekbones and an aquiline nose. There were marks at the bridge of her nose, so she clearly wore glasses at least sometimes. I noted a laptop on the side table with a pair of glasses, and smirked at the realisation I was keeping an eye out for clues and noticing small details.

"I know I'm a stranger, but I am trying to help. People want this solved, and I seem to be in the middle of it. Did you hear what happened at the farm where Simon gets the milk from?"

"I heard. Was it an accident, or is there a connection beyond the milk?"

"I'm trying to figure that one out," I admitted. "You don't mind me asking about these things? About Simon?"

"Go ahead. He's dead now, and I've already spoken for hours with the police. I think they suspect me as now I own the business, but it's the last thing on my mind. And with people coming out of the woodwork claiming Simon owed them, I can't see there being much left of it anyway."

"You aren't going to give in to those guys, are you?" I asked.

"No, as like I said, Simon's business was his. I ran this place, that's it. He would never listen, always had this wild side, and it clearly went too far. They said there was jewellery. I swear I didn't know. Simon was always doing this and that, whatever he could to make money, but dealing with those thugs is too much. Maybe if I find what they want they'll leave me alone."

"Any ideas?

"No, none. My guess is he had things at the factory, but that's ruined and it will cost a fortune to repair, so I don't know what I'm going to do. It's such a mess."

"The insurance will cover the damage. Put in a claim when you're feeling ready. The police will have a case number on file, so ask them for it and I'm sure you'll be covered."

"Yes, of course. My head is such a mess, I hadn't even thought about it. That silly man. If he was still alive, I'd kill him." Lucy's eyes became saucers and her hand slapped against her mouth, then she sobbed.

Anxious trotted over and pawed at her legs gently until she looked down. She stroked behind his ear where he liked it, almost as if she already knew.

"He's sweet. What's his name?"

"It's Anxious, and a long story."

"Another time?"

"Another time," I agreed.

Having played his part in calming Lucy, Anxious curled up by her feet and sighed happily. He always loved it when he could help people out, and I was very proud of him.

"He's adorable." Lucy wiped her eyes, brushed small hands with impeccable nails through her hair, and lifted her head, eyes locked on mine. There was a toughness, maybe even a coldness there, but kindness too. "What can you do about this? Can you get the gangsters off my back?"

"I don't see how. Maybe by finding out who did this to Simon it will help. Do you really think they'll hurt you?"

"They might. They have a bad reputation. I can't seem to think straight. I'm exhausted. Max, I don't know you, and all I heard is that you found my Simon, and you were there when the incident at the farm happened, but beyond that you're a stranger. I'm finding this very strange and uncomfortable."

"I understand. We'll go. But I am truly sorry for your loss. If there's anything I can do to help, then please come find me. I'm at Sanctuary, in a bright orange two-tone VW, so am easy enough to spot. Take care. I'll see myself out."

Lucy nodded and broke into a reticent smile, so I called for Anxious and we left her alone. I didn't like to think of her being there by herself, but wasn't sure what else I could do. I just made sure the door was closed properly and returned to the campsite to sort through all my fresh laundry.

Organising everything took a while, and yet it was relaxing and made me happy as I knew it would make life easier for a while until I had to face the laundrette again. I couldn't imagine what it was like in the winter when there would be so many more clothes and nowhere to put things to stop them getting wet. Maybe I could use the shelter and hang things to dry out of the rain but with the wind to help? I'd have to ask Mickey and Sue how they handled such things.

There was no such problem now, though, as it was blisteringly hot and about as perfect a day as you could get. I decided a nice walk on the beach would be good for me, and knew Anxious would be up for it. Once across the road and on the sand, I felt calmer immediately. There was something about the sea, the sand, and the air itself that recharged me. Was it something to do with ions?

Trev was up at his watchtower, bored as usual, and I waved at him so he waved back, tanned god that he was, looking buff and as happy as a man could be in such dangerously skimpy shorts. I wondered how he never seemed to be burned, just shone golden.

He came down the steps and we chatted for a short while, then he asked, "Did you see the cool patterns in the sand? After the rain stopped it looked amazing, but it's still impressive now. Come and take a look."

"You get patterns in the sand? You mean from the wind?"

"No, not the wind. When it's been raked smooth with the machines it's super flat, and then if we get rain you get these wicked patterns, see?"

I took proper notice of the bone dry sand and marvelled at the little splashes like miniature craters covering the beach. "What are the other long lines?"

"Oh, that's from when it gets raked clean then smoothed over. Brian used to do it, but now Jeff does it. Usually once or twice a week or more often if we get bad weather and there's a lot of flotsam and jetsam. Lots of popular beaches have it done. People expect a spotless sandy beach and it's good for the tourists. That's why it always looks so amazing. Sometimes we get whole trees brought in with the tide, or masses of seaweed. But the tractors sort it out and you'd never know it happened. It gets done very early so nobody even knows."

"It is a very pretty beach. I always wondered how some were so immaculate. You working all day today?"

"Yes, more's the pity. I wanted to come find you and see if I could help out with the investigation. How's it going?"

I began to fill Trev in on what I'd been up to, and my thoughts, and he grew more animated the more I said. But then someone shouted from the beach and I didn't get the chance to tell him about the gangsters. He raced off, looking like he was auditioning for Baywatch, then stopped when he reached the woman who had been shouting. She pointed not out to sea but across the sand to where her dog was racing around with its lead dragging behind it.

I laughed as Trev's shoulders dropped, his chance to rescue a drowning damsel in distress foiled, but then he loped after the dog anyway, chasing it to grab the lead.

Anxious and I continued on our walk and I told him he could go play once we were near the water. He stood in the shallows waiting for me to throw his ball, which I dutifully did, and the late morning's fun and games began.

The fair was in full swing by the time we'd finished at the beach, with the rides beginning to get busy, but I knew the real crowds wouldn't be around until the evening. The heat was too intense to queue to be whirled from one side to the other or be flung into the air only to have the bottom drop out of your world. Min would love it, me not so much. I smiled at the screams of people happily being terrified, and wondered if my stomach could handle any of it now.

Speakers blared all along the street that had been closed off for the day. Cheesy, dramatic monologues encouraging people to have the scare of their life, or risk limbs, hissed and crackled, or pop music at full volume interspersed with recordings of people having fun filled the air to build the atmosphere. Bored-looking young men and women sold tickets or spun people around on the Waltzer. A grizzled guy warned about removing seatbelts on dodgems. Smiling women were doing brisk business selling overpriced burgers and candy floss to children looking glassy-eyed and running amok. Happy days.

We drifted through the sound barrier and back to our pitch where I set about making lunch while Anxious relaxed in the shade of the camper. It was just a simple sandwich, but I'd got some free-range pulled pork sliced into suitably thick pieces at a local butchers, and with a generous spread of English mustard I knew it would go down a treat. A sprinkle of Maldon sea salt and it was good to go.

Frowning, I stood back and studied my creation. What was wrong with this picture?

It actually took several seconds for my brain to catch up with what I'd done, and when it did I felt close to tears. Old habits died hard, and although not consciously registering what I'd prepared, I realised that not only had I made Min's favourite sandwich in the whole world, especially with the white bread and a thick, chewy crust, but I'd made and plated two lunches.

My stomach flipped, my hands shook, and I steadied myself with the table as my legs weakened and I became light-headed. Close to buckling into a soggy, pathetic heap, I sucked in air and tried to force down a wave of emotion that threatened to crash over and utterly consume me.

Everything came back to me in a sudden crescendo almost unbearable to manage. The things I'd done, the way I'd acted, the all-consuming obsession with things I should have put second, firmly behind Min and our relationship. It was like everything I'd been containing burst from the bottle with a fast shake, the cork finally popped, and it was utterly overwhelming.

I already knew these things, everything I'd lost, but this was different, more intense, and as though the magnitude of my utter idiocy finally hit home.

All because of a sandwich.

Anxious whined from the shady spot by the campervan, and I turned to tell him everything was alright. But then his ears pricked up and he jumped to his feet before barking once and tearing away.

"Anxious, no running off!" I shouted, but the words caught in my throat as he returned with what I thought for a moment was a trick of my mind.

Min was fussing over him and laughing, her wavy blond hair looking lighter because of the sun, her tan coming through nicely, her slim figure clad in a pair of retro Adidas shorts and a simple green vest that sent my heart to aching. There was a lightness, a carefree joie de vivre that made her, at least to my eyes, almost shine.

"Are you real?" I called out as she approached with Anxious trotting merrily by her side, tail declaring his happiness.

Min stopped, put a finger to her cheek as though thinking, her eyes on mine, and laughed. "I think so. Do I look real?"

"You look like an angel," I admitted, meaning it. "You're not going to believe this, but I made you a sandwich."

"Shut up, you didn't!" she giggled, joining me in the sun shelter.

"I did, but don't look. Turn away."

With a quizzical grin, she dutifully spun, and I said, "Guess what it is. Go on. And wow, it's great to see you."

"It isn't my favourite, is it?" she asked.

"You got it right! You can turn around now."

Min whirled, Anxious ran circuits, and I pointed at the table. "Pork and mustard with crusty white bread."

"How did you know?"

"I didn't. I was on auto-pilot, probably because of the pork, and then I realised and nearly had a heart attack."

"Why? What do you mean?"

"I mean it suddenly whooshed over me what I'd... Never mind that. You came! We didn't think you would."

"How could I resist a day out at the fair? And like you said, it's only a few hours' drive so why not?"

"Exactly! Why not? And now you have a sandwich too." I grinned at Min, my anxiety vanishing.

"What are you so happy about?" she asked, hands on hips, showing off her fine legs. Legs that I recalled... "Earth to Max?" she chuckled.

"Sorry, but you look great. You been sunbathing?"

"I have. I took a little time for myself after I came to visit you and it's been lovely. Relaxing, just doing nothing, giving myself permission to take it easy. That's thanks to you and your vagabond lifestyle. You know I was jealous, so I figured why not?"

"That's the spirit. So, you found it okay?"

"Easy. Sanctuary was on Google Maps so I came straight here. And it's not hard to spot you when you have a bright orange campervan."

"True."

For an awkward moment we stood facing each other but not speaking, and Anxious sat between us, head cocked, looking from one to the other, then he barked and we both laughed.

"We're acting like we don't know each other better than anyone else in the world," sighed Min, then we both stepped forward at the same time and embraced. Min was five five and I was six one so she did as she always had and nestled into my chest. I rested my chin on the top of her head and took in a smell as familiar as Anxious' farts but much more agreeable. Essence of Min. I could have remained there for eternity.

Min relaxed her hold and her head tilted up as I moved away a little, then she stood on tiptoe and I bent so we could kiss. Brief, our lips barely touching, but it was more than enough for me to know that I would continue to fight for this woman. This beautiful, caring, kind person.

"Give me my sandwich," she growled, brushing at her lips, a frown of confusion crossing her face.

"You can even have the good chair," I offered, laughing. "Let's sit in the shade and I'll make you a drink then we can eat. What would you like?"

"If you tell me you have lemonade then I'll kiss you again," she teased, eyes sparkling.

"Wait right there!" I raced into the campervan, yanked open the fridge, and removed two bottles of lemonade I'd bought a few days ago on a whim. Now I knew why. A just-in-case because I knew she loved it on a warm day.

Kiss given, drinks in cup holders, plates on our laps, we settled down to eat our lunch. Just the three of us.

Chapter 12

We chatted about this and that over lunch, then I showed Min my various systems for washing and drying and how I'd organised everything with the large plastic tubs. She was impressed, but not surprised, as I'd always been rather fanatical about things when it came to the kitchen.

Once everything was cleared away, we settled down for a while in the sun, Min stripped to her bikini, me trying not to ogle, which was difficult, nigh on impossible. The afternoon was glorious, with a gentle breeze washing over the campsite to stop us overheating, but not enough to ruin the perfect day.

Min had missed the storm entirely. Seemingly, it had been very local and she hardly believed me when I explained how it had been earlier when I recounted my visit to the launderette.

"Are you ready to fill me in on what you've been up to? You told me about the murder and what you found, but what else has happened? And who do you think did it?"

"What makes you think I have a suspect? Why assume I'm involved at all?"

"Max, I know you, remember? So don't play games with me." Min shielded her eyes with her hand as she leaned forward, her body glistening with the sunscreen.

"Am I that obvious?"

"You like to know things. You need control. Which is why this new life is so good for you. It's letting you relax and go with the flow more. But you notice small details, want things just so, and that's a needed trait for a sleuth. You've always been excellent at puzzle-solving, so who do you think could have killed that poor man?"

"There are two bodies now," I said. "It's a long story, so let's go back to the beginning."

Min was all ears as I spent the next hour going over everything, leaving nothing out, with as much detail as I could recall. When I was finished, she was quiet for a long time, then threw up her arms and declared, "I have no idea who did it!" and laughed.

"Neither do I, but there's something obvious that's being overlooked and then everything will fit into place."

"It sounds like it was probably the gangsters. They want their stolen goods back from Simon's partner, and most likely they killed him when he didn't have their money or refused to hand over the jewellery. That makes the most sense."

"Yes, but when they were at Lucy's they didn't sound like they'd killed him."

"But it could be another dodgy character. If he was involved with men like that, I'm sure there are others."

"True," I admitted. "But Lucy is suspicious too. Although, I don't think she has it in her to kill Simon."

"You never know. She will own the ice-cream shop now. It's a decent business."

"It is. But there's also the competition. Chester, the owner of Lovely Stuff, has been after the milk for his ice-cream for ages, so maybe he decided to off Simon and hoped he'd get the milk."

"Yes, but he wasn't up at the farm when the farmer was killed. What was his name?"

"Brian's the farmer who owned the place, and Jeff works there. He's the one who was in the workshop when I arrived. He didn't hear a thing."

"Could Chester have been up there without Jeff knowing and argued with Brian then done something in the milking parlour?"

"No, because he was at his ice-cream shop working."

"What about Jeff then?"

"He was distraught and swore someone had done it. He wouldn't say that if it was him."

"Okay, maybe the death at the farm was an accident and Chester the other ice-cream shop owner killed Simon."

"It's possible, but somehow I think the deaths are linked. It's too much of a coincidence. And the woman at Chester's shop said she was with him at the factory the morning Simon was killed. She seemed quite annoyed that people were suspecting her boss."

"Then that leaves us with who?"

"Nobody," I said, deflated by the realisation. "Wait! There are the women who work at the factory. I told you about the lady at the launderette, right?"

"You did. So maybe this Amber did it to get away from her clingy mother?"

"They didn't seem like that though. They were happy to be together, a team, but if what Ruby said is true, then maybe that's motive."

"And what about your new bestie? This lifeguard, Trev?"

"What about him?"

"You've discounted him, haven't you?"

"Never thought for a moment it could be him."

"He was on the beach, so could have easily done it. If it was early, nobody would have seen and he could have returned to his watchtower and waited for someone to find the foot. Um, didn't you say yourself that it was Trev who suggested you try to find this big crab?"

"Yes, but I'd suggested going to the rock pools."

"But he led you to a specific spot to find the crab, and that's right where Simon was. That's suspicious, you have to admit that."

"I really hadn't considered him, and although, yes, you're right, there is no way Trev did it."

"Why do you say that?"

"You haven't met him yet, but when you do, you'll understand why."

"Okay, let's leave that to one side for now. What about this H character? Some old hippy dude who doesn't want his way of life challenged and hates bad sorts in what he feels is his town. Maybe he'd had enough of Simon and his dodgy friends. They argued, something happened, so he killed him."

"Again, you haven't met H. If you do, then you'll realise he most definitely isn't the type. And why would he chop Simon's foot off?"

"Why would anyone?"

"Good point. I think it's time to admit that I'm stumped and maybe this is best left to the detectives. How about we just forget about all this and enjoy ourselves? After all, there's a reason why you came, isn't there?" I waggled my eyebrows, causing Min to giggle, but then she frowned. "What's wrong?"

"You aren't getting any ideas, are you? I wasn't sure whether to come after last week when I rushed off like that. I know I was sending mixed messages, but you understand that nothing's going to happen, don't you?"

"Of course I do. I hadn't changed the sheets or anything."

"You liar!" Min punched my arm playfully, then her hand remained resting on my shoulder. "Max, I do love you, and part of me wants to jump on you right now—"

"I won't try to stop you."

"—but it's not a good idea, and it will make things even more complicated than they already are. Deep down, neither of us wants that kind of stress. Can we just be friends and enjoy each other's company?"

"We most certainly can do that. I've got everything I need for dinner, so how about you help me with that and after we eat we can go to the funfair? Sound like a good plan?"

"It sounds perfect, but can we go to the beach first? It's only early, so let's do that then come back and cook."

"Deal."

Anxious, although dozing, was now beside us, eyes boring into our heads, willing us to stand and take him on the promised walk. How he always heard, I never knew, but any mention of activity and he'd snap out of his sleep and be there in a flash.

Once the van was locked up, we headed out to the road where Min marvelled at the funfair and had to hold herself back from jumping on the nearest ride. She made me promise we'd try everything that evening, and I wondered if dinner was such a good idea or I should starve myself so I wouldn't barf over the other riders.

Anxious was in his element on the beach, and tore off to chase seagulls. The large birds easily outsmarted him, taunting the little fella by swooping low and calling for him to give chase, which he did happily.

Min clapped her hands with delight; she really loved Anxious.

"Do you miss him?"

"So much. I wish he was with me at home, but I know he's happier with you."

"He loves you, and always will," I said, hoping Min knew what I meant by that.

"And I love him. But I understand he needs to spread his wings and have his freedom. It's what he needs. But maybe one day we'll be together again. Just not in the foreseeable future as it's time he found himself and time I learned how to relax and put myself first."

"Are we still talking about the dog?" I laughed.

"What do you think?" Min danced away, smiling, and beckoned me to give chase, so I ran after her as she jogged backwards then stumbled and fell.

"Are you okay?"

She was laughing as I hauled her to her feet, then said, "Fine. I need to wash this sand off. Dare you to come for a swim."

"I haven't got my costume. It's alright for you, but I'm in shorts."

"Then who cares? They're just shorts. Come on, let's do it."

"Okay, you're on."

Min ran off ahead with Anxious barking excitably by her side, so I joined them and she grabbed my hand. Without stopping, we raced into the water and splashed as we waded out then released each other and dove into the water.

I surfaced with a gasp to find Min beside me, grinning, her hair plastered to her face and shoulders.

"It's freezing!" she squealed.

"So cold. People come for a swim first thing in the morning. They must get pneumonia."

"I think you get used to it. Once you're in, it's not so bad."

"No, then why are your teeth chattering? And why can't I feel my toes?"

"Argh, ugh, what's that?" Min splashed in a panic and tried to swim back to shore, but then a dark shape surfaced in front of her and she screamed.

Anxious' head popped out of the water and he grinned his dopey smile, then paddled around us both, excited by the commotion.

"You should have seen your face!"

"He scared me. I thought there was a shark." We swam to the shallows and stood up to our waists. "Maybe that's what got Simon? Could it have been a shark?"

"I think there would have been bite marks if that was the case."

"So how was he killed? Was it just blood loss?"

"No, he had a nasty wound on his neck and... Hey, let's not talk about it, okay?"

"Sure, Max, whatever you say."

"Are you staying in, or aren't you a fan of being blue?"

"Not a fan."

Min teased the hair from her face and we waded to shore with Anxious beside us, then sank into the sand and let our legs get washed by the gentle tide as it lapped against us, the water feeling positively warm after our swim.

We sat there for a while, then rinsed in the sea to get the sand off before walking along the beach, smiling at people playing with their children, laughing at the dogs digging like crazies as they joined in with the kids burying their parents in the sand.

Once the little guy was suitably tired, we returned to the campsite and showered. Sand remained, as it always did, but at least the parts most liable to chafing were spared from further discomfort.

We then settled into a routine as we made dinner. Tonight was to be a simple but always tasty winner of sweet-chilli prawns and pasta. It was light, which I thought was ideal because of the evening's planned festivities, and it didn't take an age to cook. Min was already itching to have at the rides, and I knew an extended slow-cook one-pot wonder was not going to cut it.

We ate it with a simple side salad and leftover bread from lunch to soak up the amazing broth, then cleaned up to ensure no bugs were attracted.

"Can we go now?" asked Min the moment the last of the cutlery was safely stowed.

"Give me time to sort out the bed before we go. I don't want to get caught out again. Um, what's the plan? Are you staying, or are you going home tonight? I can sleep outside if you want. Give you some privacy."

"I'll stay, if that's alright? But I don't want to put you out."

"It's no bother. I love it up on the tiny platform right by the roof." I smiled, but Min frowned. "Sorry, that came out wrong. Honestly, I don't mind. I was trying to be funny, but it sounded petty. I'd love you to stay."

"Then how about we come back, have a bottle of wine, and sleep under the stars? It's so warm anyway that it'll be nice, and we can see the sky."

"That sounds like a wonderful idea. I won't bother with the bed then."

"Oh, maybe get it ready just in case I happen to change my mind in the middle of the night." Min winked, then laughed.

"Sure, just in case."

After I wrangled with the Rock-n-Roll bed and ensured the floor was free of hazards, I locked up and we headed back out onto the road to enjoy all the fun of the fair.

Min was like an excitable kid as we approached the blaring speakers, flashing lights, and the screams of people being flung about in utterly unnatural ways. She'd always been this way, and loved the funfair more than just about anything. It was the one time when she was utterly carefree and immersed in the moment. Like it was her release mechanism, a way to destress and let the pretend terror eradicate pent-up damaging emotions.

I adored seeing her so uninhibited, and it was why I'd hoped she'd come, but hadn't really expected her to.

Anxious was not a fan of the lights or noise, and he'd gladly remained at the campervan where he was no doubt recovering from his day's exertions.

First, we went on the Waltzer. I just about handled it. Then we went on something despicable where you were strapped into a cage and spun left, then sharply right, then flung around and up only to plummet back down. I almost vomited.

Next up entailed us being locked in a two person metal bubble and catapulted out on octopus-like arms then whizzed back into the centre before being flattened against the sides of the cage as we flew out towards the grinning, smug people watching, their dinner safely in the bottom of their stomachs where it belonged.

I'd definitely had enough.

"I'll just watch for the next one," I gasped as I gripped a railing and tried to keep my food in place.

"Spoilsport," teased Min as she dashed off to pay for a ride that seemed to consist of just being taken up high then dropped like a rock.

I took several photos as she raised her hands in the air and screamed along with everyone else, but as she staggered from the ride looking a very peculiar colour, even Min admitted, "I think I might be getting too old for this. I don't feel right at all."

I took her arm and refrained from saying anything too smug, so suggested we get a coffee and take a seat to recover. She didn't need much convincing.

It was fun watching everyone on the rides, and the atmosphere was buzzing. Nothing like a single day for a fairground to get packed. Children wanted to go on every ride, much to the consternation of their parents as some had to have an adult and all were overpriced, but there were plenty of things for the younger ones to do, too, and the smiling faces were a delight.

I spotted Trev wandering around in his usual get-up of shorts and not much else, although at least he wasn't wearing his lifeguard ones, so called to him and waved. He came over, flushed and grinning.

"Trev, this is Min, my best friend besides Anxious, and my ex-wife."

"Nice to meet you," said Trev, shaking Min's hand but frowning.

"I get it, it's weird, right?" laughed Min. "I bet you thought Max was making it up and we hated each other really."

"Why would he think that?" I asked.

"Because that's what is supposed to happen, silly."

"I did think you might have been exaggerating," admitted Trev. "But it's nice to meet you. Are you visiting for the day, or are you going to join Max for his vanlife adventure?"

"Just for tonight. I'll go home tomorrow. So, you're the lifeguard Max has been telling me about?"

"Did he call me the buff one?" grinned Max, bouncing his pecs.

"He might have," chuckled Min, her eyes fixed on his tanned chest. "But you do know you're also a suspect? I told Max that it was probably you as you led him to the rock pool where the body was, and that's very suspicious. You had the means as you were on the beach, and it was rather convenient that you took him right there. Was it you, Trev?" Min leaned in close and hissed, "Are you the killer?"

Trev blanched, pecs forgotten, his tan fading until he appeared almost ghost-like. "It wasn't me! Don't tell the police or I'll be in real trouble! I swear I didn't do it. No way are you pinning this on me. Tell her, Max. You gotta tell her I'm innocent."

"Relax, you muppet," I laughed. "Min was pulling your leg." I turned to her and admonished, "You shouldn't scare him like that. Look at the poor guy."

"Sorry about that, Trev. I was just messing around, honest. I don't think you did it."

"Wow, good. You had me going there."

"Or do I?" demanded Min, jumping up and getting in his face. "Admit it, you did it."

"No, I didn't. I promise it wasn't me!" he squealed.

"Stop winding the poor man up, Min."

"Sorry, I couldn't help it," she laughed. "You know I was joking, right?"

"Um, yeah, sure," gushed Trev, taking a seat as he was so shaken. "Wow, you're kinda intense. Dude, she's terrifying," he told me.

"Just my little joke," said Min, scooting Trev over so she could sit between us.

"Not funny." Trev wiped his brow with his forearm, then pointed and said, "But here's a real suspect now. Look at him."

Chapter 13

We watched as Simon's ice-cream competition, Chester, shuffled through the crowds looking morose, worried, and annoyed. He was taking his time, eyes darting, as though looking for someone.

"He's so dodgy," confided Trev.

"Is he into illegal things like this Simon was?" asked Min.

"Not that I know of. But he looks the sort, right? It's just his demeanour. I bet it was him."

"It can't be, remember? He was working when the cows killed Brian, and he was making ice-cream the morning Simon was found."

"Maybe he slipped out to do a spot of murdering," suggested Trev.

"People were in the shop constantly when Brian was killed, so it wasn't him. And his employee said he was at his factory with her from early in the morning the day Simon was found."

"I don't think he killed Simon anyway. He's just an obnoxious guy, but he's not a criminal. He's just sour about the milk. Ha, get it?" Trev jabbed me in the ribs, eyebrows raised.

"Yes, I get it," I laughed, shaking my head.

"Who's he talking to?" asked Min.

"That's the woman who worked for Simon, and those are her daughters. Remember, I told you I'd met them at the factory and they were very upset. And I spoke to Ruby this morning."

"You didn't tell me that," huffed Trev.

"I haven't seen you since. I'll fill you in tomorrow, but it was most likely nothing. Are they friends?"

"Not that I know of. Chester doesn't really have friends. He lives for ice-cream and money. But look at them. He and Crystal, that's the mum," he explained to Min, "seem pretty tight."

"Maybe he's offering them all jobs."

"Maybe, but I bet he's got an ulterior motive."

"Which is?" I asked.

"The secret recipe, of course. He's wanted it so bad for so long."

"I never knew there was a secret recipe," Min grumbled. "That's important."

"Didn't think to mention it," said Trev. "Everyone wants it. There are other ice-cream places here, you know? We have loads, but Simon and Chester are the main players. But there are plenty who want Simon's recipe."

"Maybe he's trying to get it off Crystal?"

"She would never tell, but I doubt she knows. It was super secret stuff."

"Crystal, Ruby, and Amber help make the ice-cream," I told Min. "Trev, surely they'd know all the ingredients?"

"Up to a point, but Simon always added something extra. Look, maybe I'm wrong, but as far as I'm aware, he was the only one who knew."

"I bet his partner knew," said Min. "Maybe it was her after all, and now she plans to sell the recipe to the highest bidder. Max, you should ask her."

"I can't exactly just bring that up in conversation. By the way, will you sell me the secret recipe so I can flog more cones than you now your beloved is dead? Think that would work?"

"You'd find a way. You're good with people."

"Maybe sometimes, but not with stuff like this. No, I'm coming to the conclusion that none of them did it and we need to start all over again."

"Mate, just leave it to the police. They'll figure it out." Trev stood and studied the throng, then said, "Right, I've got things to do, ladies to chat up. See you guys around." Trev hurried over to a group of three young woman he may or may not have already known, and soon was deep in conversation with them, flexing his muscles.

"He's quite a character," noted Min.

"He sure is," I laughed. "I like him and he's funny. Smart, too, for someone so young."

"You make it sound like we're really old. We're only, what, ten years or so older than him?"

"Maybe for you, closer to seven for me."

"Now I do feel old," Min grumbled, but she was clearly excited and having a great time. "Are you going to buy me candy floss?"

"Sure, anything you want."

We weaved through the buzzing crowd, the energy building the darker it got. The lights strobed, casting everyone in ghostly white one moment then fiery red like demons the next. At the kiosk, I bought Min a candy floss but forewent one myself as I found it way too sweet. As we turned, I found DI Julia Bennet with Jeff, her godson, waiting in line.

"Hi. Didn't expect to see you here," I said, genuinely surprised.

"What, detectives aren't allowed to have fun?" she asked with a raised eyebrow.

"I thought it was against the law," I joked. "Min, this is Detective Inspector Julia Bennet and her godson, Jeff. He's from the farm," I reminded her.

"Lovely to meet you both. So sorry about what happened," she told Jeff.

"Thanks. Nice to see you too. It was a terrible thing, and poor Brian didn't deserve to go out like that."

"He didn't," agreed Julia. "But we'll find out what happened."

"Someone killed him," insisted Jeff. "The same person who killed Simon."

"Let's not start on that again," huffed Julia, her ample frame wobbling.

"I'm telling you, someone tampered with that gate and knew what the outcome would be."

"Wouldn't that make you a prime suspect?" asked Min, always rather blunt at times.

Jeff's mouth opened and closed, his colour rising, then blurted, "Don't be daft!"

"She got you there," chortled Julia, then beamed at Min. "So, you really are called Min, eh? Max and Min, the Efforts." She shook her head in wonder.

"Yes, it's all true. We have the worst names of a couple ever. Ex-couple, I mean." Min hid her embarrassment at her slip of the tongue behind the pink candy floss.

"It's sweet. And, Min, you do have a point. Maybe I should start investigating you, eh, Jeff? See what skeletons you have in your closet? More like metal tool cabinet as you're always in that workshop."

"You're welcome to look, but you know I thought the world of Brian. Even if he was a grumpy old duffer most of the time."

"At least now you'll get what you deserve," said Julia.

"I hope so," Jeff agreed.

"What's that?" I asked, intrigued.

"Oh, nothing, just family things. Personal stuff," said Julia. "I'm still not convinced it wasn't an accident. Brian was getting on and had a few issues lately, so this isn't a surprise. And we found nothing out-of-the ordinary in the milking parlour, so we're at a loss."

"Something will turn up," said Jeff, nodding.

"Well, nice to see you at last, Min. Please tell your ex-husband to bugger off and that I politely request I never see him again. He has a nasty habit of showing up whenever there is a crime, and it's becoming suspicious. Maybe you're who I should focus on, Max."

"Me!? I solved the last crime."

"Doesn't mean you didn't commit this one," she warned.

"I'll try to keep him out of trouble. But Max has an eye for detail and it's details that solve cases, isn't it?"

"Yes, it is. Very astute."

"Just one more thing?" I asked.

"Fine." Julia sighed and crossed her arms, looking menacing as the lights turned green.

"The woman from Lovely Stuff, Chester's assistant, said he was with her the whole morning Simon died. Did you look into that?"

"Yes, we did, and he was. He's a grumpy, but timid man, and Simon dwarfed him. Even without the alibi, he's not much of a suspect. It had to be someone strong and big to get Simon down to the water."

"Or they had a boat," piped up Min.

"That doesn't narrow it down much when you're at the coast," snapped Julia. "Are we done here? I'm trying to console my godson and at least have a little fun."

"Yes, sorry," I said.

"Me too," said Min.

We left them to get their candy floss, and moved to a quieter, and darker, spot at the very edge of the fair to get some space.

"She's quite a character. Very flamboyant with her bright Caribbean dress. She's big too. Very intimidating."

"She is, yes. But I like her, and she's given me some good advice. Julia doesn't mind me looking into things as long as I don't tread on her toes and ensure I stay out of her partner's way."

"So, all the suspects have come to the fair," noted Min as she tore at her candy floss and swallowed with a grin of delight.

"Some of them, but not all. Simon's partner isn't here, or I haven't seen her, and certainly not the gangsters."

"It's most likely them or another gang. Normal people don't chop feet off. That's a gang thing. Like a warning to others that they need to toe the line. Geddit? Toe the line."

"Min," I admonished, "That's in very bad taste."

"Sorry, you're right. I'm getting carried away with this. It's more remote for me than it is for you. Was it awful?"

"It was, without doubt, the most surreal thing I have ever seen in my life. It just didn't make sense, you know? Like it had to be connected to the rest of a person. But it wasn't."

"You poor thing. Come on, let's go have a ride on the dodgems then we can go home."

"Now, dodgems I can do."

After three goes, Min had finally had enough so we walked back to the campsite arm in arm, chatting happily and thoroughly enjoying ourselves.

Anxious was ecstatic to see us and stuck to Min like glue even when she dashed off to the toilet. When they returned, she said he even went into the stall with her and that was why she took so long—Anxious sat there staring at her the whole time and put her off.

I poured the wine and we settled in the chairs, enjoying the sounds of people being terrified on the rides and chatting quietly as things slowly settled and the lights went out. By eleven, all that could be heard were the quiet murmurs of people on the campsite, and the evening took on a magical feeling as though Min and I were the only people in the world.

At midnight, I unrolled the sleeping bags and we huddled together underneath the shelter with Anxious between us like it used to be for years—I slept better than I had since the first night I found myself in bed without Min.

I awoke with a sick knot in my stomach, expecting her to be gone like last time, but she was still there, fast asleep, with Anxious curled up beside her head on the pillow. I got up quietly and used the facilities, then put the kettle on for coffee.

"What time is it?" asked a sleepy Min as she stirred.

"Just gone seven."

"Needed a pee, did you?" she smirked.

"Yes, but I didn't have to get up in the night for a change, which was great."

"I slept so well too. Haven't had such a good night's sleep for over a year." Min frowned as she mulled that over, then said, "Gosh, I hadn't even thought about that until now, but I don't think I've had a great night's sleep ever since we..."

"I'm the same. I feel more rested than I have in ages."

Min grinned, then spluttered as Anxious licked her face happily. "And a good morning to you, too, Anxious. Look at the state of the pillow! It's muddy."

"And they're new ones. I forgot to bring pillows with me."

Anxious jumped up and went crazy licking Min's face, tail like it had a life of its own. Seemed I wasn't the only one to be pleased she'd stayed.

"Hey, stop it, you silly dog!" laughed Min.

Anxious gave her nose a final oh-so-sticky icky-licky, then skipped off to relieve himself. Sometimes, it's hard not to be jealous of your dog.

"Ugh, so gross," she giggled as she wiped at her face and tried to tame her mussed-up hair. After losing the battle, she sat up and tried to squirm out of the sleeping bag without unzipping it, something she had always done for some reason. It didn't go well and she toppled sideways, tangled in the fabric, arms pinned inside.

Anxious returned from the bushes to find Min rolling around like a fish out of water. The cheery guy was only too happy to oblige with what she was in desperate need of, so attacked the poor, defenceless woman by jumping on her and barking excitedly between more face licking.

"Stop it!" Min giggled, writhing to get away but sending Anxious into a frenzy of happiness.

I laughed at their antics, the morning perfect, and hoped it could last forever.

"Why don't you ever unzip it?" I accused. "It's easy to get out then."

"It's my thing. I refuse to use the zip on a sleeping back to either get in or out. You have to slide around. It's loads easier."

"Yes, you've certainly mastered that particular challenge," I agreed as Min's head disappeared into the sleeping bag to avoid Anxious. He wasn't going to let her get away with that, though, so dove in after her. I could trace his route around the sleeping bag as she battled with the happy pooch before his head finally emerged with Min's, tears rolling down her cheeks as she laughed manically.

"I... I really need a pee. Help me out of here before Anxious makes me wee in the sleeping bag."

"Anxious, come on, leave Min alone before she wets herself," I said, then clicked my fingers. He gave her a final slobbery kiss before bounding away and sitting, tail swishing, eyes glued to Min to wait for whatever the next fun game might be.

I hauled Min out by grabbing under her arms as she sighed with relief to finally be free, then squirmed the rest of the way out, jumped to her feet, and declared, "See? Easy!"

"Yes, it looked it. You better get a move on, as everyone else is waking up and you might have to queue." I pointed up the field where various campers were rushing towards the toilet and shower blocks with towels and wash bags.

"This is what I hate about camping. We need our own bathroom."

"I'll see what I can do," I said, trying not to laugh as she panicked then ran off with Anxious right beside her.

When they returned, I gave Anxious his breakfast and handed Min a coffee.

"I got in just in time," Min gushed, her cheeks flushed, but grinning like the cat who got the cream. "I hate public toilets though. There needs to be a better system."

"Like what? Personal bathrooms for everyone right on your pitch?"

"That would be amazing! Yes, let's suggest that."

"I'll get right on it. Can I have my coffee first?"

"Just the one cup then sort it out."

"Got it."

Min and I smiled at each other, the old banter and easygoing nature of our relationship having returned to how it used to be. She was a great friend, and I treasured these moments.

"What's the plan for today then?"

"I'm not sure. When were you heading off?"

"That depends how awesome the day is. I'm in no hurry if you don't have anything you need to do. I'd love to just hang out on the beach and do absolutely nothing. Read a book, sunbathe, maybe another swim? If that isn't too boring?" She shivered at the thought of the water, then added, "Maybe not a swim. A paddle might be better."

"I can do all of that, sure. And it won't be boring. It never is with you. It's called relaxing, and it's not something either of us have done enough of."

"No suspects to interview?" she asked.

"Don't make fun of me. I think I've spoken to everyone who might be involved, but that doesn't mean I've spoken to the killer."

"Course you have, silly. Max, I bet you have spoken to the killer, and once the information percolates into that clever mind of yours, you'll realise who it was. Maybe it was one murder, maybe it was two, but you'll figure it out."

"You seem very certain about that. Why?"

"Because you always solve the problems you face. You can work out individual ingredients from a dish, which is why other chefs hated it when you went to their restaurants."

"They did," I agreed.

"And whenever we lost things, or had an issue with something, you would go over events until you found the answer. It's how you're wired. So, I'm sure you'll figure this out. Maybe a relaxing morning on the beach is what you need to let this sink in. I bet by tomorrow you'll be revealing the killer and annoying the detectives."

"Let's hope so."

Chapter 14

We got our things together then took Anxious to the beach. He was in seventh heaven, incredulous about the amount of walks he was having, the number of times he got to play on the beach, and meeting more people in the last week than he had the entire previous year. It made my heart soar.

Min and I spent an amazing few hours doing nothing but throwing the ball for our insatiable dog until he finally relented and curled up between us after ensuring he did what all dogs adored by getting sand on and in everything.

We chatted, but not too much. Rather, we mostly sat and people watched, soaking up the glorious heat of the morning.

Closing in on lunchtime, Min asked me a very important question. "Are you enjoying this? Isn't living in the van more hassle than it's worth? No space, no garden, no big TV or all your things? Do you regret it, or think you'll come back home soon?"

"Wow, that's a lot of questions," I chuckled.

"Sorry, but I'm interested."

"So far, I'm really enjoying it. It's a challenge, and yes, it's hassle not having much room, but in some ways I prefer it. It gets me outside more, like so much more, and when I'm not outside I'm more connected to everything because so much of this life involves not being stuck inside. Maybe because I can see the weather through the windows, or maybe because I know I have to do things like shopping, sorting out water, laundry, and endless other tasks that I feel much more a part of the world. Does that make sense?"

"Absolutely. You can't shut yourself away like you can in a house."

"As for TV and other things. I don't miss that. I have my laptop, I have a seat, a bed, even a little table, and when the weather's nice I'm out here. I don't think I'll be renting or buying a house any time soon, Min. Don't get me wrong, after even just a few days I'm finding plenty to complain about, and maybe come ask me the same questions once it's winter, but I'm actually looking forward to the challenge. And I think that's a big part of this vanlife. It is a challenge. You have to fend for yourself much more, and plan ahead. I like it."

"Then good for you!" Min smiled, but there was a sadness and hesitancy behind her eyes that she couldn't mask from me.

"What's wrong?"

"It's just you might be so far away. Probably for the next month or two you'll be a few hours drive, but what if you're the other side of the country? Max, I miss you."

"And I miss you. But you did visit me the day after I left. We go weeks without seeing each other usually. Sometimes months."

"But this is different. It's as though you've truly gone. Sorry, I'm hardly making sense to myself, so this must sound like gibberish."

"Not at all." I took Min's warm hands in mine and looked into her eyes welled with tears. "Min, I get it, okay?" She nodded, mute. "It's difficult for both of us. There's still a connection, that's obvious, because we're holding hands on the beach, but we have heaps of history and not all of it's good. Thinking about us being together again is a huge decision, maybe the biggest one we'll make in our lives after what we've already been through, so I don't expect you to tell me everything about how you're feeling, or for you to even truly understand how you do feel. And that's okay."

"It is?" Min squeezed my hands.

"Sure. Of course. It's complicated. I get that. You want to be sure, and you don't want to get hurt again or hurt me. You have to be a hundred percent certain, and right now you aren't. It's fine. I get it."

"But I am certain, and that's what's so worrying. And why I can't commit. I need to be Min for a while. Not Max and Min. Just Min. Find myself again. Gosh, that sounds beyond cheesy, but it's true. I need to do what you're doing. Fend for myself, make my own way, and find out what I'm made of deep down."

"But you're sure about us?" I asked, grinning.

"Max! Okay, cards on the table time?"

"Shoot."

"I love you, but I don't always trust you."

It was like a hammer blow to the chest; I felt the pain so deeply I gasped.

"I'm sorry, I'm so sorry. I didn't mean it in a bad way. I didn't mean you aren't trustworthy. How do I explain this? What I mean is that I need to be sure that you've changed, and that's going to take time. You've only just begun to sort out your life and future, and all that's happened has been leading up to your dramatic attitude switch. I need to know it's permanent. Not that you'll go back to being consumed by work and fixated on stuff that isn't important to us as a couple. As a family. Understand?"

"I do," I admitted. "And you're right. Min, I promise you I'll prove that I'm a better man. But it will take a while as I'm still working through things. Take your time, be sure. But you can trust me. I realise how I was, but that's done with. I feel like I've found a true home now, and yes, I'm aware that sounds nuts as I have no permanent address. But this has awoken something in me and I won't go back to how I was. Join me when you're ready, or let me know you want me to come back."

"I couldn't take this away from you. That's another thing to consider. I won't do that."

"Min, don't you get it?"

"What?"

"You're my true home. Wherever you are, if I'm there with you, that's enough. More than enough."

"Oh, Max."

"Hey, you said you wanted all the cards on the table. Now you have them. It's nothing to be sad about. It's life. I'm having a blast, and I'll cope, you can be sure of that. Just like I know you will. But to share my life with you is a blessing, and one I always cherished. If we get another shot, that will be incredible. But you do what's best for you. Don't feel bad about being undecided. I know it's a huge step and incredible pressure."

"I don't want to screw this up, you understand? We've got on so well in recent months, and you're my best friend, my only true friend, so to risk losing even that..."

"So just forget about it," I said brightly.

"Max, I can't."

"Of course you can. There's no hurry. Min, I'm thirty-three, you're thirty-six. We have what, hopefully at least another fifty years or more on the planet if were lucky? We're friends. You can come and visit or stay as often as you like, but as for the rest, just let it play out however it will. Go with it and take the pressure off. But let me tell you one thing."

"Sure."

"You will be mine again."

Min laughed, I winked, then we embraced. When we broke apart with a nod, something had changed, and my words had clearly made an impression. Min looked like a weight had been lifted from her shoulders, and I knew we'd be alright.

We had a paddle to cool down and to throw the ball for Anxious now he'd had a rest, then decided to go and make lunch.

Chatting happily as we returned to the campsite, our conversation was cut off when we heard the commotion and noticed the flashing lights.

"What's going on?" I asked Trev, Mickey, and Sue who were at the edge of a crowd of people talking loudly. Several police cars and an unmarked vehicle I recognised as the one used by the DIs had their lights flashing and were making a real display in the usually peaceful field known as Sanctuary.

"They're arresting H, and he isn't going quietly," said Mickey, shaking his head sadly.

"He's such a sweetheart too," sighed Sue.

"The cops have it in for us," noted Trev with an angry tone.

"Why would they arrest him?" I wondered, not understanding.

"I'm guessing they believe he killed Simon," said Mickey sadly. "But it can't be him. He's as kind-hearted a man as you'll ever meet. No way he chopped off Simon's foot."

"That's right," hissed another man.

Others agreed, and it began to get loud and ugly as the crowd surged forward towards the detectives and several officers surrounding H. He'd backed up to his home, a large, old blue bus he'd been living in for years at the top of the field, and was refusing to cooperate.

"You can't arrest me for this! Why would I kill him? You're not making any sense. I hardly even knew the guy. It wasn't my scene."

"Found it," shouted a policeman as he exited the bus and held up a large plastic evidence bag with what appeared to be a small machete inside. It was covered in blood. "And I got the missing latch from the gate too. A double murder!" he crowed, holding another bag aloft.

Another officer exited the bus, with yet another evidence bag, and declared, "A lot of cash for someone with no job," the money strobing under the glare of red and blue lights.

"That's not mine! Oh, c'mon, you guys, as if? What, I just left the murder weapon and incriminating evidence lying around for you to find? I'm not dumb. None of that's mine."

"Then you can tell it to us down at the station," said Malc, as monotone and disinterested looking as always.

"Just come quietly and we can sort this mess out," soothed Julia, putting her large arm out to grab his wrist.

H backed away further, eyes darting, and screeched, "I'm innocent," before the arresting officers managed to cut behind him and snap the handcuffs on. "Hey, that's not fair! This is a total set-up. Why am I being framed? And I swear I don't know anything about any stolen jewellery. This is so dumb."

"What's that about jewellery?" asked Min.

"They searched his bus and found a load of watches and other things," said Mickey. "That's a fair amount of money too. Looks like it's Simon's judging by the way they were acting. Must have been a tip-off, but not sure why they think it's his."

"I was here first and heard," said Trev, eyes sparkling. "They found a wallet too. Simon's. It was in another bag."

"So now they think he stole dodgy jewellery from Simon and killed him?"

"Looks that way. H isn't into any of that, he's a right hippy. This is so obviously a set-up it isn't even funny."

"I guess the police have to follow up on leads, and if there's evidence like this they're going to take it seriously," noted Min.

Mickey and Sue turned to her and Mickey frowned. "Who are you?"

"Oh, sorry, I haven't made introductions. Mickey and Sue, meet Min. Min, meet Mickey and Sue."

"Ah, the ex-wife," said Mickey, grinning.

"Hi," said Min rather awkwardly.

"Ignore him," said Sue with a scowl for Mickey. "He can be rather blunt at times. Nice to meet you. You were at the other place, too, right? We didn't come say hi as you were having a picnic, but lovely to meet you."

"You too. So are they going to take this H away?"

"I guess," shrugged Trev.

"But it's so obviously been planted. Who in their right mind would keep the murder weapon and the evidence?" sniffled Sue.

"It's alright, babe, they won't pin it on him. He'll get out, you'll see." Mickey draped his arm around Sue's shaking shoulders and drew her in tight.

"I know the DIs. I'll go and have a word," I said, then squeezed through the crowd that had become increasingly restless now H was in handcuffs.

By the time I reached the front and stepped out into the open, H was being marched to the nearest police car.

"Julia, did you get a tip-off?" I asked as I approached.

"It's DI Bennet, and I'm DI Anderson in case you'd forgotten," barked Malc, emotional for the first time.

"Sorry, I didn't mean any offence."

"Malc's just rather annoyed by everyone acting like we're the bad guys," grumbled DI Bennet with a sigh. She turned and addressed the crowd, and asked a question nobody could answer. "Would you rather we didn't take lines of inquiry seriously? That if we found evidence of a suspected murder and criminal activity we just let the suspect go? No, I didn't think so. If H is innocent, then he will be found innocent, but he needs to come in for questioning. Got it?"

With mumbles from the crowd, but nobody blatantly trying to interfere, Julia nodded to the officers and they got H into the car. But not before he looked at me with pleading eyes then said softly, "Help me, please?"

I nodded, as what else could I do? Malc sidled over to their car looking exhausted, and I asked Julia, "Is he okay? He looks ready to collapse, and he's not normally emotional."

"He bottles it up then blows sometimes. And, Max, in case you hadn't noticed, we're in the middle of a murder investigation. Possibly a double murder. It's tiring work. This is different to last time in Rhyl. There are more suspects and many more reasons why Simon is dead. We didn't have much to go on last time, but this time we have, if anything, too much. It's a headache for us both."

"I understand. I'm assuming you got an anonymous call about H?"

"Yes, what of it?"

"Just that it's very convenient, right?"

"Of course it is. But we had to follow up and we had to arrest him. If you know H, then you know he's a nice guy but not the sharpest pencil in the case. If he were to commit a murder, then this is exactly how I'd expect him to behave. He's too "chilled" for his own good."

I nodded. "What happens now?"

"He's been arrested under suspicion so we'll question him. Forensics will check over his bus, the bagged items will be checked, too, and we'll take it from there. He won't be charged with any murders until I'm satisfied. Understand? I'll do my best." Julia drew me in close and whispered, "If you know anything, then now's the time to tell. We had an agreement, remember?"

"I was coming to call you. Lucy had a visit from the local heavies. A young lad in a tracksuit and a guy with a burn on his face. Lucy said you'd know them. She didn't even want to say their names."

"I know them," spat Julia. "The man with the scar is an ex-con with a terrible history and an even worse attitude. The youngster is his kid. One of them. He has quite a few from quite a few women. He's not a good father or a good criminal. We'll pay them another visit. They're already on our radar. Will Lucy press charges?"

"What do you think? And they didn't touch her, just threatened her. They said Simon owed them money and they wanted it or their gear back. I'm guessing the jewellery you just found." I pointed to the constable carefully placing the evidence in the car then closing the boot.

"We've got ourselves a real mystery here, Max, and I don't like it one bit. People are playing with us, trying to cover their own backs, and it gives me a bad feeling in my lovely lady parts."

"What!?" I spluttered.

"Hey, we're all adults," smirked Julia. "Be careful. What were you doing at Lucy's?"

"I wanted to pay my respects, tell her what happened. Thought it might help."

"And did it?" she asked, eyebrow raised like she was aiming to get it off the top of her head.

"Actually, a little. Poor thing is really shaken up. It's a big shock."

"We spoke to her a few times, and yes, it's a lot to take in. She stayed out of Simon's more secretive life as far as we can tell, but she's still a suspect, Max, same as several others. Lucy isn't the most agreeable person, which makes it harder to get her to talk, but she seems genuine. Now, I have to get on."

I nodded as Julia turned to go, but Anxious whined and his ears dropped. She turned back, looked down at him, and smiled. "Sorry, my little buddy, was I being rude? I have a lot on my mind, but that's no excuse." Julia bent with a grunt and Anxious was instantly happy again. She patted his head, stroked his back, then shoved off her thighs with her hands to stand. "I gotta lose some weight," she grumbled.

"He likes you. So do I," I grinned.

"Don't push your luck, Max," Julia warned, then smiled.

"Yes, DI Bennet, sorry."

Julia laughed, then waved over her shoulder as she went to join Malc who was waiting impatiently by the car.

Chapter 15

Soon enough, everyone left, leaving the residents to gossip and complain, but the wind was already gone from their sails. Nothing but confusion, shock, and suspicion remained. Those who knew H well clearly didn't believe he had anything to do with it, and even a newcomer like myself found it incredulous that anyone would keep such evidence where it could be so easily recovered.

"He's obviously been framed," said Mickey as we walked back over to the campervan he and Sue lived in.

"But why?" asked Trev.

"It's obvious, isn't it?" said Mickey as he sat in a chair and indicated we should sit too.

"Not to me," admitted Trev.

"Because someone's got it in for him. He lives a free life, is unconventional, and his parents have all this land that he lets us use. It rankles some people that we live differently to others. It's always been the same."

"That's not reason enough to pin it on him," I protested. "And let's not forget that whoever did plant the evidence is the killer. Unless the police find that the jewellery is his and the machete isn't the murder weapon."

"I bet it is," said Trev. "So Max is right and the killer planted it. It's not somebody who hates travellers or unconventional people, it's someone with a real grudge."

"Or," said Sue, rather shyly, "they didn't have a grudge at all and just figured he's an easy target. They might have just thought it would be a breeze to get him into trouble and it would take the heat off them."

"That's a great point," I agreed, smiling.

"Yeah, well done, babe," said Mickey, impressed.

"It makes sense," said Min. "It's an easy way to distract the police, but also to ensure they know there were two murders. Max said they weren't certain about the farmer's death being a crime, but this confirms it. They're linked now, and that's precisely what the murderer wants. They don't want there to be any doubt."

"That's so smart," said Trev, full of admiration.

"Think about it," continued Sue. "People come and go all the time. H is often wandering about away from here, and he's at the beach a lot, so it would be easy to slip in and plant the evidence. Maybe they didn't even know him. It's probably the gangsters Simon had dealings with looking for an easy way to avert suspicion."

"I met two of them earlier," I mumbled, unsure whether I should tell them.

With gasps, then plenty of encouragement to tell all, I gave them the story. When it was over, I expected insight or shocked reactions, but it was eerily silent.

"What's wrong? Why are you all so quiet?"

"Mate, you got off really lightly there. You're a lucky man," spluttered Trev, suddenly overcome with a coughing fit.

"He's right," agreed Mickey with a sympathetic smile. "We've travelled these parts quite regularly and everyone knows about Jackson and Brody."

"Which one's which?"

"Jackson's the older guy, Brody is his kid. Nasty as his dad and enjoys hurting people. You should steer clear."

"I will. Damn, I'm hungry."

"We already ate, or we'd offer you something," said Sue.

"That's fine. I have food at the camper."

"I'm starving too," sighed Trev. "I came back for lunch then got distracted by all the action."

"Me too," agreed Min.

"I'll make us a sandwich," I told Trev. "If you fancy?"

"Mate, that sounds awesome!" He grinned happily, rubbing at his enviably flat stomach. Did the man never wear a T-shirt? I guess I wouldn't if I had a body like his.

We left Mickey and Sue to it and weaved our way through the campsite to Vee. People were buzzing with the excitement, and rumour and gossip were rife. Seemingly, everyone had an opinion, everyone knew who the real culprit was, and everyone felt they should regale the campsite with what they "knew" to be fact.

Lunch wasn't very impressive, but the bread was good, the Cheddar excellent, and a tomato chutney I'd picked up at a deli was delicious, so we had a reasonable Ploughman's lunch and ate it on the grass.

"Do you eat like this every day?" asked Trev, eyeing up the last of the cheese.

"Pretty much, why?"

"Because it's amazing. How do you make it so nice?"

"It's bread, cheese, and pickle," I said, nonplussed.

"But if I make a sandwich it's just a flat, limp mess."

"Max has a real gift for making even the most basic ingredients shine," said Min with pride.

"Wish I could cook properly. It's the one issue with being here on your own. I'm not the best in the kitchen, and I have even less space than you, so it gets to be a problem. I eat too much junk."

"And it costs you more than making proper meals from scratch. Trev, the basics of cooking a decent meal are simple. I'll show you later on if you like? I'm doing one-pot cooking every night if possible. It's a challenge I set myself. Later, I'll show you a great recipe and you can follow along, okay?"

"Really? That sounds great. Thanks. Should I bring anything?"

"Nope, you're my guest. I have everything I need. Or, I will once I find it all."

"It takes a while to get this life figured out," laughed Trev as he grinned then nabbed the last slice of cheese once Min and I nodded it was okay. "It takes most people weeks, if not months, to put a proper system in place. You've been doing this for what, a few days?"

"Not long. A few days, yes."

"Then you're doing great, Max. You have your outdoor kitchen, which all the long-term van lifers set up if they're staying anywhere for more than a day or two. You learned that quickly. Everything slots into place slowly. Don't beat yourself up over it." Trev kicked back in the chair with his legs stretched out in front of him, a goofy smile on his face. "This is the life, eh?"

"Sure is. So, it took you a while to get organised?"

"Mate, I'm still not organised," he giggled. "There's always something that needs doing, always a way to maximise space, arrange things a little better, stuff you want, stuff you realise you don't need, and it never stops. The secret is to go with the flow and not let it bother you, but for it to be part of the enjoyment. You're casting a smaller footprint. Yes, we drive smelly vehicles, but it's nothing compared to the impact we'd have living in a conventional home."

"That why you do it? Lower your carbon footprint, tread lightly on the earth?"

Trev fidgeted with the hem of his striking red shorts, then smiled as he brushed his sun-bleached hair from his tanned face and grinned, his teeth shockingly white. "I wish I could say yes, but the honest answer is that I just love this life and I like not having to spend all my money on a house or flat. It's less stressful, and I'm not so good under stress."

"You're a lifeguard! That's stressful."

"Yeah, but in a different way. It's not hanging over me, you know? I don't worry as much. I'm a natural worrier, so this suits me. I know myself well enough to be sure this is the right thing for me. Who knows what the future will hold, but for now this is perfect."

"Then you're a smart guy, Trev," said Min. "Most men your age haven't got a clue what they want out of life. So long may it last."

"Thanks. So, let's get serious. Max, why are you so into this? The murder, I mean? Why are you trying to figure it out? You don't owe anyone anything. You never even knew Simon. Or the farmer."

"No, I never knew those men, but this is my personality. I can't leave a job half finished. It's who I am. This life is allowing me to ease up, to take a step back, but I suppose I'm still a person who hates unfinished business. I have an eye for detail, is what it boils down to. I find the flaws and fix them. That's what it takes to be a top chef."

"And a good sleuth. So, who do we think did it?" Trev leaned forward, eyes locked on mine, nodding his encouragement for me to continue.

"We? So we're going to solve this, are we?"

"Mate, course we are. We found Simon, you found Brian, and now they've arrested H. He's a great guy and we have to clear his name. If that means catching the real killer, or killers, then that's what I want to do."

"It's what I've been trying to do."

"So, who could it be?"

"Okay, here's what I have so far," I began, feelingly excitement build despite the serious nature of the crimes. "We obviously have the gangsters, Jackson and Brody. They were putting pressure on Lucy earlier. But that might be too obvious, and why would they kill a farmer?"

"If he was killed."

"Exactly."

"So who else? Oh, I know. How about Chester from Lovely Stuff? He's getting all the ice-cream business and he and Simon hated each other."

"Yes, definitely a possibility. But what about Lucy herself? Maybe she'd had enough of Simon getting up to no good and killed him so she'd inherit the business."

"Could be. But she doesn't seem the type."

"No, she doesn't, but still, it's a possibility. Or it's as the police are saying and H did it."

"No way! You don't believe that, surely?"

"No, I don't. Okay, so we have gangsters, rival ice-cream shops, maybe a disgruntled partner, or maybe Jeff, the man who worked up at the farm did it."

"Why would he? And he's the one who insisted Brian's death was no accident."

"I have no idea," I admitted.

"Jeff's a good guy and you know his godmother's that DI, right? The big woman?"

"Yes, I know. What do you think about the women that work at the factory? They seem nice, but they're an odd bunch. I bumped into Ruby at the laundrette and she said her sister, Amber, has been wanting to escape for a while now. Could there be a motive there?"

"You really aren't from around here, are you?" said Trev. "They're a pretty ferocious bunch, sure, but super tight. No way they'd kill Simon and trash the factory."

"Maybe Amber would if it meant she could leave. Losing her job means she can break free and go her own way without so much grief from her mum and sister."

"Nah, they aren't like that."

"So who does it leave us with?" I mused.

"A right mystery, is what." Trev frowned as he rubbed at his face. His watch caught his eye and he panicked. "I need to get back! My lunch break is over and I'll be in trouble. See you later?"

"Yes, see you later."

"It was great to meet you, Min. You sticking around? We could do with the help."

"I'll be leaving later, and I'm sure you two will figure this out. But be careful, both of you. This is a serious business."

"But we have to help H out. And it's not just that."

"What else?" asked Min.

"Pride," said Trev, head down.

"Pride?" I asked.

"In this place. I know it isn't the best beach in the world, or the most stunning views, but it's home and I like the people. We deserve to know it's safe. We need answers.

H has done plenty for this community, but so have a lot of other people. We need to ensure they feel safe, and we need to help stop anything else bad happening."

"I understand, and don't worry, we'll figure this out. We might pop to the pub in a bit, so if you can get time off come and meet us. It feels like we're getting somewhere with this now."

Trev nodded, then raced off towards the beach. I sank back into my chair to think for a while. Who could have done this? And why? What piece of this puzzle was missing? What was the main ingredient that would consolidate everything and make sense?

"He really does love it here," noted Min as she began piling up the plates and cutlery.

"He sure does. He's rattled, even though he's trying to act brave. It must be harder when you know everyone. He doesn't want to think badly of anyone, but now he can't stop thinking of people as suspects."

"That would be awful. Maybe you should go and talk to the police and tell them more about the gangsters. They shouldn't be allowed to threaten a widow like that, and what if they go back?"

"I already told the DI. She'll look into it. And although Lucy was shaken by them being there, she didn't seem that cut up about Simon being dead. There's something going on there."

"She probably hated that he was involved with them."

"I'm sure she did, but there's also the fact that she has a lot to gain by Simon's death. Maybe this was her way of getting him out of the picture. She might have paid someone to kill Simon so she could inherit the business and not have to deal with all the dodgy characters he was involved with."

"That doesn't explain the farmer."

"No, it doesn't," I said glumly. "What a head-scratcher."

"I know!" exclaimed Min, eyes alight with a fire of conviction.

"What?"

"The farmer wasn't killed at all. But there's so much gossip about it that the killer decided to plant evidence so it seemed like a murder. It will confuse everyone and they'll be looking for a motive that doesn't exist. It's perfect. It will make the police doubt that the gangsters are to blame, as what would they want with an old farmer who just sold nice milk?"

"You could be right. Maybe we should go and have a drink and forget about this for a while. Something might turn up if we give it time. I feel bad for H, but there's nothing we can do at the moment. Julia will go by the book and ensure the case stays open until she's satisfied."

"That poor man. It must be awful to be arrested like that. He'll be so scared."

"I know I would be."

"Where shall we go for a drink?"

"How about that pub we passed earlier? We can sit outside and watch the world go by for a while. Inspiration might hit."

"I guess I better get changed after I do the dishes."

"I'll sort out the dishes. I have a system. You get ready, but it's just the pub so no need to dress up."

"Max, I have my bikini on. I was going to just slip into my dress and that's me done."

"No shower?" I asked.

"A freezing cold shower in a room where people are peeing? I'll wait until I'm home, thanks." Min fake-shuddered then grinned at me.

"It's not so bad once you get used to it. But yes, a shower at home will definitely be nicer."

Once the dishes were cleaned and everything was put away, I had a quick wash, ran my hands through my hair, slipped on a vest, and we were good to go.

Chapter 16

We settled ourselves outside the pub where we could watch people strolling along the beach, the various picnic benches, tables, and chairs busy with tourists. With a glass of wine each, it was lovely to just sit back and relax.

"I feel like I'm on holiday," I grinned, content despite the upset at the campsite.

"Me too. Although, I suppose I am. You aren't though. Shouldn't you be doing something?"

"Nope, no need."

"You don't miss work?"

"Sure I do," I admitted. "It's taken some getting used to, but I'm getting better at not always being busy."

"It suits you. You're more chilled than I've ever known you to be."

"And I intend to carry on being chilled." I studied the other customers, and my smile faded when I spied Barry perched on the low stone wall with a half pint of Guinness untouched beside him, his camera trained on us.

"Look, it's that guy, Barry. He's definitely spying on me. He's got a camera pointed at us."

Min followed my gaze and we watched as Volvo Barry lowered his camera, hastily grabbed his drink, and sipped to hide his embarrassment.

"What's his game?"

"No idea, but I'm going to find out once and for all. Can you wait here?"

"Of course. Don't get too angry, though, he's clearly just odd."

I weaved through the laughing tourists and stood in front of Barry, my arms crossed. "What's this all about, Barry? This isn't funny anymore. I keep finding you spying on me and it's beyond unnerving. Why are you so interested in me?"

"I'm not," he stammered, glancing at his camera.

"You are! Did you take that photo up at the polytunnels? The one with Anxious tearing at that woman's jeans?"

"Me? Why would you think that?" His voice was so high-pitched I was amazed he didn't shatter his glass.

"Because I saw you there."

"You're mistaken. I'm just a bird-watcher having a nice holiday. I can't help it if you're in the same place as me." Barry downed his drink, settled the glass, then raced off without another word.

I watched him hurry along the road, then duck out of sight. "That guy," I muttered, then returned to Min.

"Well?"

"He denied following me. Said it was just a coincidence."

"Maybe it is. Why would he be interested in you?"

"I have absolutely no idea."

"Excuse me," asked a smartly dressed woman I judged to be in her mid-fifties. Her dark hair was cut short at the back and left long at the front, parted to reveal intense brown eyes with heavy eyeliner. Her three-quarter black trousers showed off impractical shoes for walking far, and she seemed rather flustered because she wore a long-sleeved purple shirt of material too thick for the weather.

"Yes?"

"Would you mind if I sit? There are no other chairs and I really need this." She raised a large glass of wine, the bubbles catching the light.

"Sure, be our guest." I shifted my chair so she could join us at the small table.

"I don't normally intrude like this, but I have to get off my feet."

"Shoes pinching, are they?" asked Min as she smiled then indicated the chair.

"Like you wouldn't believe." The woman sank into the chair gratefully, then took a sip of her wine and her shoulders drooped. "Oh, that is so good. I needed it. Sorry, it makes me sound like a drunk, but I don't normally ever drink during the day."

"Me either," admitted Min. "Had a tough day?"

"The worst. Very upsetting and stressful. Do you mind?" Our guest indicated her shoes as she slipped them off, her toes red and looking like they would blister.

"Hey, I feel overdressed not wearing my Crocs," I laughed. "Barefoot is even better though."

"I'm so silly. I had an important appointment, and I got up at stupid o'clock to ensure I wasn't late and dressed like an idiot. I don't know what I was thinking. All the upset, I suppose. I'm strictly a jeans and T-shirt gal usually, but thought I should make the effort. I've only worn these shoes once before for a wedding, and I didn't even consider the heat when I put this stupid shirt on. I don't have anything else so now I'm stuck sweltering."

"Sounds like you've had a stressful day," I said. "I'm Max, by the way. And this is Min."

"Nice to meet you. I'm Rosa. Are you on holiday?"

We explained our situation without going into detail, and she took it in her stride. No judgement or questions, just smiles and brief words of understanding. I got the impression she'd been through enough of a personal journey in her life to not be phased by other people's situations.

"So, what brings you here? You seem to know it quite well. Are you from around here?"

"I'm local, but moved away for university and only ever came back to visit. When my mum died, I guess I stopped coming quite as much, and over the years visits became less and less frequent. I didn't see eye-to-eye with my father, and it got harder over time. He was a tough man to love and very set in his ways, but I did love him. Now I can't tell him that." Rosa dabbed at her eyes, but then flung her hair back and smiled wanly. "Sorry, you don't want to hear about my troubles. It's done. I came for a will reading. It was very old-fashioned and stuffy in a musty office. But it's over now and I'll head home after this. Don't worry, I'm getting the train so I'm not drink driving."

"Sorry to hear about your loss. Your father, I assume?" asked Min.

"Yes, and now there's talk about it being murder. It's shocking, and I just don't know what to think. He was a hard man and tough as old boots, but he had no enemies and I can't understand it at all. It seems like there might have been foul play, but the police are still looking into it."

Min and I exchanged a glance and Rosa must have picked up on our silence as she asked, "What? Do you know something?"

"I'm assuming you're talking about Brian, the farmer?" I asked.

"Yes, how do you know? Oh, I get it. Small town gossip. If you're staying at the campsite, you would have heard."

"Actually, I was there when he was discovered," I admitted.

Rosa's eyes widened as she gulped her wine, then insisted, "Please, tell me everything."

"Hey, guys, room for one more?" asked Trev cheerily as he dragged a chair from another table and sat down with a sigh.

"Couldn't keep away, eh?" I asked.

"Got someone to swap the rest of my shift with me. I decided to take you up on your offer. If that's alright?" he asked, looking from me to Min. "If I'm interrupting, I can go."

"No, we already invited you, Trev. It's fine. I know you're upset about H and all that trouble, so please join us."

Trev nodded with a smile, his eyes darting to Rosa. "Hi."

"Hi."

After introductions were made, Trev settled himself and we quickly got him up to speed on who Rosa was. Trev became animated, and was clearly desperate to ask her endless questions, but I shook my head in warning and he sank back into his chair and waited for my lead.

"So, you were there when Dad was found?" encouraged Rosa, her drink forgotten. "Jeff called me after it happened and explained that he thought someone must have done it on purpose, but that didn't seem right at all. Who could do such a thing?"

"Maybe it was Jeff," blurted Trev. "Maybe he wants to ensure he has a nice future if he gets a girlfriend? Settle down, have kids."

"Trev!" I warned.

"No, it's okay, and he was the only one there. But now they have evidence from this H character. Is he guilty?"

"It wasn't H," insisted Trev, arms crossed over his bare chest.

"And it wasn't Jeff. He's been working there forever, and although he and Dad didn't always get on, he loved Dad in his own way. He's as stuck in the mud as Dad was, though, and is disappointed not to be carrying on as normal, but I've been trying to get Dad to change the farm for years. In the will, he left a personal note for me, saying he was sorry he never agreed to the changes I suggested, but that I should go ahead and do them. Make the place something special, you know?"

"Sure, that makes sense," said Min. "Why do you say Jeff couldn't have done it though?"

"Because it's his world. All he ever wanted was to work on the farm and carry on like it had always been. And besides, didn't he insist it was murder when everyone else said it was an accident?"

"He did," I conceded. "He was adamant. But he had no alibi. Just said he was in the workshop."

"With that damn radio blaring, no doubt," said Rosa with a curl of her lip. "Jeff isn't my favourite person, but he and Dad were very close. He's like a brother to me. Just a very annoying one. He was like a son to Dad. I've often thought he would have preferred to have Jeff than me. They were close."

"So you'll keep him on?"

"Of course, but there will be big changes. Jeff came to the will reading, but he left as soon as he could. He wasn't happy about it, but he already knew I was getting the majority of the business."

"He thought he might inherit it?" I blurted, recalling the conversation with Julia and her hinting about her godson getting what he deserved now Brian had passed.

"No, and he saw the will a few years back when Dad updated it. It was private, but Dad left it out and Jeff confronted us both about it. He was annoyed, as I think maybe Dad had been playing him along, promising he could have a larger share or something, but he's known for a few years that I would inherit the lot. I think Jeff might have tried to invest more into the business, but they clammed up the moment I raised the subject. Why do you ask?" Rosa's hand shot to her mouth as her eyes widened, and she whispered, "You don't think he did it? He wouldn't. What do you know?"

"All I know is that his godmother said something to me about Jeff getting what he deserved now, that it had been promised to him. But I guess he never told her that things had changed, or he'd been duped into thinking he'd inherit the farm."

"It was him. It has to be," squealed Trev.

"But he's the one who insisted it was murder," said Min, confused. "Why would he do that?"

"I have a very good idea why. Rosa, you're sure about this?"

"Yes, positive. Jeff's known for years I'd inherit. I told him today I'd keep him on, but that I'll be moving into the farmhouse and overseeing everything. It can't be him. It just can't be."

"Where is he now? Do you know?"

"He said he was going to the bank then back to the farm. I think his godmother and her partner were meeting him there."

"Do you know why?"

"Something about the way the gates work, I think. He said they had some questions and he was meeting them. I'm not really sure. He wasn't happy with the will reading, but he knew what it said already. This just made it official, and he's still a part owner after Dad sold him a stake a long time ago. But I have final say, and I won't let him change my mind."

"Okay, we need to go," I told Min and Trev. "Right now. Where's the bank?"

Trev explained where it was, so we said our goodbyes to Rosa and I stood.

"What should I do?"

"Nothing. Do nothing. This might be a false alarm, but maybe not. Just, er, don't go up to the farm."

"I can't stay here alone. Not if he's the killer. What if he finds me? What if he's watching?"

"He won't be. But I'll stay," said Min, smiling wanly at me.

"That's a good idea. Then you'll both be safe. Go inside the pub and don't leave until we come back. Can you do that?"

"Sure, we can drink wine," laughed Min, but with an air of concern.

Suddenly, this had become very real for everyone.

"Oh, thank you so much. But I'm sure you're wrong. Jeff would never hurt Dad. They were so close."

"I hope you're right, but there's certainly something wrong with this whole picture. It's time to get answers."

After a kiss from Min—just for me—we dashed off with Anxious trotting beside me as we hurried across the street and back into town a little where the bank was. When we arrived, it was to see a very red-faced Jeff storm out of the door, nearly knocking over a man entering. The man swore at Jeff but I don't even think he heard him, then Jeff jumped into his Land Rover and tore off with a squeal of rubber.

"We need to follow him," I said. "Right now."

"This doesn't make any sense," said Trev. "Why would he kill the old man if he knew he wasn't getting the inheritance?"

"So he could pin Simon's death on someone. And now H is the prime suspect."

"Unless Rosa is lying and she had something to do with it," said Trev, frowning. "She might be setting him up."

"There's only one way to find out. Come on, let's go."

"What about Min? What if it's Rosa?"

"It's not Rosa. She was beyond squeamish about a blister. She's not about to chop someone's foot off."

We nipped through the gate at the bottom of the field and got into Vee. I drove frustratingly slowly through the campsite until we hit the road. Then I floored it.

Which meant we moved a little faster than we had been, but weren't about to break any land speed records.

"Do we need anything?" asked Trev, eyes dancing, face and neck flushed. He wasn't even bouncing his pecs.

"Like what?"

"I dunno. Weapons? Call the police maybe?"

"Hopefully, Rosa was right and the DIs are up at the farm now. She said they were going to meet Jeff."

"I was sure it was Simon's wife. She seemed the type. Or maybe Chester, the dude with the other ice-cream shop."

"He had an alibi, remember? And Lucy wasn't happy with Simon, I'm sure of that, but kill him? No, this is all falling into place."

"How do you do this, Max? How do you figure it out?"

"Because I listen, and understand what pieces fit where. Plus, Rosa said Jeff knew about the will."

"But pretended he didn't? I don't get it."

"You will. He's probably been stewing for years about not getting his inheritance, and saw a way out. Maybe he didn't kill Simon, but he saw his opportunity to pin Brian's murder on whoever did, so planted evidence. Maybe the machete is nothing more than a ruse, a way to get the catch from the gate into H's place, but we're going to make him talk."

"You can't just make someone talk."

"You can if you're clever, or they're dumb. And my guess is that Jeff's not too smart if he's involved in this. Look, there's the Land Rover and the DI's car. At least we know they're all here."

Trev jumped out and sorted the gate while I drove through and parked. I killed the engine, unfastened Anxious, and we stood by the VW for a moment, then approached when the DIs and Jeff emerged from the milking parlour.

"Time to finish this," I muttered.

"Unless they're all in on it and we end up trampled by cows," whispered Trev, shivering.

Chapter 17

"Max, what are you doing here?" DI Julia Bennet frowned as she took in the sight of me and Trev.

Malc took a step away from her and Jeff, who looked smart in a dark suit, white shirt, although no tie. The only thing that gave him away as a farm worker were the Wellington boots he wore because of the muddy yard.

"You don't know when to give it a rest, do you?" Malc spoke in his usual bored monotone, but there was an underlying warning there. His eyes were cold and his body language was if not aggressive then certainly not his usual, "I couldn't care less," stance.

"It's okay, Malc," soothed Julia with a hand to his arm. He turned to check with her and she nodded, so Malc just glared at us.

I felt incongruous in my cutoffs and Crocs, and Trev looked plain wrong in his red shorts. We were not dressed for a farm, that was for sure.

"We saw Jeff coming out of the bank in town earlier, and it was something that Trev here said that got me to thinking. Plus, we met Rosa. You know her, I assume?"

"Thinking can get you into all kinds of trouble," said Malc, a definite threat to his tone. "You've been told enough times already to leave this to the professionals."

"Rosa, Brian's daughter?" asked Julia, frowning.

"Yes. We just left her."

"And you've done nothing but arrest poor H," blurted Trev.

"Because he had the murder weapon in his bus," said Julia with a weary sigh as she wiped at her face with a handkerchief. "What do you want? What's this about Jeff and the bank? What business is it of yours?"

"Why were you at the bank, Jeff?" I asked.

"That's none of your business. You need to leave. I've got things to do. The cows need milking soon, and you know what they're like if they don't get sorted."

"They get antsy and trample people to death? Is that what you're going to tell me?"

"What is wrong with you? What do you want?" Jeff tugged at his shirt collar and undid a button, clearly uncomfortable in smart clothes.

"Why were you at the bank, Jeff?" I asked again, feeling the nerves rise.

"You were at the bank?" asked Julia. "You said you were going to see the solicitor about your share of the farm."

"His share?" I asked, like I didn't know the story.

"Max, this is none of your business," warned Julia. "But if you must know, my godson has been a partner in the farm for a long time. Jeff was always promised this place by Brian, as his daughter had no interest, so now he owns the lot. Not that there's much to it, and it certainly isn't what you'd call very profitable. I understand that could be seen as a motive for murdering Brian, but Jeff's wrong about that, I'm convinced. Brian's death was accidental."

"We do alright, Julia," muttered Jeff. "And yes, I went to the bank to sort out a few things. What of it? I spoke to the solicitor with Rosa, and it's done."

"And then what, you going to put your feet up and relax?" I asked.

"As if! This farm is a full-time job and you know it. The cows take so much time and then there's the deliveries and everything else around here."

Anxious whined, clearly bored, so decided to go and play with his new friends and raced across the yard to say hello to the two sheep dogs over by the workshop.

"But you will sell, right?" asked Julia, looking rather confused.

"Tell her, Jeff. We already know, but go on, tell her."

Jeff's eyes darted from me to Trev, who had his arms folded across his chest in a way I guess he thought was intimidating, and finally to Julia. He sighed, then his shoulders sank, and he admitted, "Brian didn't leave the farm to me. All these years, the endless hours I've put in, and he lied. He left it to his daughter, and she's got big plans. She wants to expand the herd, open up a farm shop of all things, get rare breed animals, and even open a petting zoo. Totally change things and modernise. She's moving into the house."

"But he can't do that! He promised you. Are you sure?"

"I'm sure. It's done. I don't own any of it beyond a small slice. He promised me. Swore that the work I'd done would be worthwhile, and when he passed it would be mine. More, he said that when he retired he'd let me run things how I wanted and be the boss. It was all lies."

"How do you know this?" asked Malc, glancing back to me and Trev.

"Because he saw the will, right, Jeff? You knew ages ago that Brian had frozen you out. That he was lying about leaving it to you. He spun you a yarn, told you what you wanted to hear so you'd keep working for him. That must have rankled."

"I don't know what you're talking about! I only heard today at the solicitor's, like I told you."

"No, you didn't. We spoke to Rosa and she explained everything. She seemed nice. You're up to your neck in this."

"She was lovely," agreed Trev. "She told us that you saw the will and got into an argument."

I glanced at Trev, surprised he was being so cool. "That's right," I agreed. "You pretended like you didn't care once you'd calmed down, and just carried on working here the same as always."

"That cow can't keep her damn mouth shut," spat Jeff, then realised what he'd said and forced himself to relax. "I was disappointed, yes, but what of it? I thought after all the decades I've worked here the old git would keep his word, but I should have known better. He was never a nice guy, always grumpy, never gave me a Christmas bonus or a kind word for all I did, and he lied to me!" Jeff's fists bunched and his cheeks burned crimson, but he stood his ground.

"Godson, what does this mean?"

"I think we know what it means," drawled Malc, nodding to me. I returned the expression and glanced at the filthy old Land Rover, warning that Jeff might try to make a run for it. Malc shifted his position to intercept if need be, but Jeff didn't seem like he was about to run.

"It means I was cheated, that's all!" shouted Jeff. "Cheated out of a crappy business that only survived because of dumb milk!"

"But it's the best," said Trev. "Made me the man I am today." He bounced his pecs and watched his muscles dance with immense pride.

"It's just milk!" screamed Jeff. "Everyone always goes on about it, but it's only milk. We look after the girls, and yes, the grass is good quality, and yes, we grade the feed properly, but it's still plain milk."

"You need to calm down," ordered Julia, sweating badly and looking, for the first time, rather unsure of herself.

"Calm down. Why should I? I get dressed up only to confirm that I'm getting nothing! Rosa inherits the lot and wants to change this dump beyond recognition. The bank won't lend me any money to start up on my own, and I'll probably become destitute."

"But you won't, will you? And my guess is, you asked for a mortgage because you suspected you'd be told to leave the farmhouse. I assume you got turned down? Banks are loathe to lend money at the moment, but you already suspected that, so made other plans. And besides, you don't make enough money here to buy an equivalent home." I said.

Jeff's head snapped up and he locked dark, angry eyes on me. "What's that supposed to mean? I just told you what happened. And why are you still here?" he raged.

"You know why. Tell your godmother now, and don't make it any harder than you have to."

"Max," sighed Julia, "I think I know where you're heading with this, but we've heard enough. Yes, you're keen to get justice for Simon and possibly Brian, but it's best you leave. Jeff might be angry, but he didn't do what you're insinuating."

"You should hear him out, Julia," said Malc softly. He confronted Jeff and lifted a finger, then pointed at him. "You too. Any attempt to run off and I won't take kindly to it, understand?"

"I can do what I want. I'm not under arrest."

"Nobody said you were," soothed Julia. "Malc, what's going on?"

"Don't play dumb, Julia. It doesn't suit you," said Malc, deadpan. "We know that Max and Trev are saying that Jeff killed Simon and dumped him down at the beach. And I'm guessing Chester had something to do with it?"

"Yep," agreed Trev, back to having his arms crossed, stance wide. I think he was going for a cop look, but he looked more like a lifeguard who'd taken a wrong turn.

"What do you know that I don't?" asked Julia as she wheezed, her colour brightening.

"It's making sense now, and it's pretty obvious if you think about it. Okay, there are some things I don't understand, but I get the feeling our amateur sleuth is going to fill in the missing pieces, right?"

"Maybe," I admitted. "Here's what I think happened, and I suppose it's easy enough to confirm some of it." I took a deep breath, then went for it. "Jeff had a meeting with Simon up here, most likely in the workshop."

"That never happened," snapped Jeff.

"It will be easy enough to check for prints, and my guess is they'll be all over the workshop. Your workshop that has a surprisingly clean floor."

Everyone turned to look at the hulking building, then Jeff turned back and mumbled, "That doesn't prove anything. Maybe he was here, maybe he wasn't. Maybe Brian had him up here. Doesn't mean I was involved."

"No, I think you were. And you weren't alone, were you? You had help with this. More than just help. I'm right, aren't I?"

"You're just making this all up!"

I ignored Jeff and continued. "What I'm assuming is that Simon was already in trouble with the gangsters, Jackson and Brody, and you both knew about it. You knew he couldn't sell the goods he was supposed to, and they wanted their money, so you both took advantage."

"Why would I bother doing that? What could be in it for me?" asked Jeff with a happy sneer, thinking he'd tripped me up.

"Money, of course. A partnership. You and your partner planned it all out. You both knew that Simon was in serious trouble and might even decide to leave, so you made him an offer. You'd bail him out with the gangsters if Simon agreed to close up shop for good and hand over his recipe for the ice-cream. That's the secret to his success, I'm guessing, not the milk. That's just what everyone believes."

"That's getting pretty far-fetched, Max," wheezed Julia. "All this over a secret recipe?"

"Are you okay?" asked Malc with concern.

"Fine. Just need to sit for a moment. It's the angina, or something I ate. All this stress." Malc helped Julia over to the wall outside the milking parlour and she sank onto it gratefully, then thumped her chest. Her colour eased off and she nodded that she was feeling better. "Carry on."

"You had Simon over a barrel and blindsided him with what you knew. Maybe he agreed, maybe he didn't, but whatever the outcome he ended up dead."

"This is utter nonsense. I'm not listening to another word of this." Jeff began to storm off, but a thick, tattooed arm shot out and clamped down on his equally meaty wrist with a grip that was no match for his.

"You stay right there and let them finish. If even part of this is true, then you are in a world of trouble. Godson or not, I won't tolerate this."

"Get off me!" Jeff bucked and twisted, but Malc took his other arm and held him fast.

"Try it again," he hissed, "and I'll cuff you. Max, make this quick."

"Either Simon agreed or not, but either way he was killed. I expect he agreed, but then maybe Brian overheard something and came into the workshop and everything unravelled."

"That didn't happen."

"Okay, then how about this? Maybe Brian didn't hear you arguing, but Simon was still murdered. There will be his blood in the workshop, Jeff, so there's no point trying to lie. Anxious went crazy in there, remember? I assumed it was the food in your lunchbox, but it wasn't, it was the blood residue on your very clean floor. I should have guessed."

"Even if there is blood, that doesn't mean I did it. It could have been Brian, or someone else."

"How could you?" wheezed Julia, shaking her head in sorrow.

"Whatever. You can't prove anything, and whatever evidence might be in there is circumstantial. I've learned a few things over the years from you, Godmother. It'll never stick."

"We're detectives," she said softly. "We'll tie up the loose ends and you will admit what you did. It's over."

"Not quite," I admitted. "Either Jeff or his accomplice killed Simon because he didn't agree to the terms, or they thought they could do better with him dead and keep the jewellery and money."

"I swear I didn't kill Simon. We were just going to make the deal," Jeff blurted. "Simon said he'd let us pay off the debt and have the whole business, but then Chester went nuts and swung for Simon with a pipe. Simon tried to run, but tripped, so Chester grabbed an old machete from my workbench and slammed it down on Simon's foot, chopping it off. Then he killed him. He was crazy."

"And then you took him down to the beach with you and did the usual clearing away, levelling the sand with the machinery, and dumped him," suggested Trev.

"Yes, okay, I did. But I swear I didn't kill him. And I didn't touch Brian, even though I've wanted to kill him for years. Brian just died, and I knew Julia and Malc were coming that afternoon so I took the latch from the gate thinking it could be used to fool everyone. The deaths were linked, so what would it have to do with me? Especially as I was the one insisting Brian was murdered."

"I knew it," said Trev smugly.

"You liar," I hissed. "You're going to pin this on Chester? I don't believe you."

"It's true. We could have had what we wanted, but Chester still wasn't happy. He was out of control and moaning about not having the recipe for the ice-cream and that was the whole point. The man's obsessed with the stuff. I tried to stop him, but he insisted on going to the factory to find it, so I went along, knowing we had to get the stolen goods and money anyway. Chester tore the place apart, but I was smart." A sly look came over Jeff as he confided, "I found the jewellery and the money, but more importantly I found the recipe in a hole under the filing cabinet. I let Chester have the cash and dodgy gear, I didn't want any part in that really, but kept quiet about the recipe. We got out of there before anyone saw us, and I came back up here."

"Chester trashed the factory looking for it?" gasped Trev.

"Yes, but he didn't get what he wanted. The idiot's obsessed with his business. He's not right in the head."

"How could you?" sighed Julia. "You're like a son to me. I looked out for you all these years. Your parents will be so disappointed. You're everything to them."

"Things got out of hand," protested Jeff. "We were meant to just be doing a deal with Simon to get what we wanted. Chester is the one who went too far."

"What were you getting out of it again?" asked Trev, confused.

"A business. I needed something. There was nothing for me here. Once I realised that, I had to find a way to make some proper money. I knew I'd have to leave the farm sooner or later. With Simon out of the picture, we were going to make a fortune. Chester and I talked in the pub and we came up with this idea to squeeze Simon out and take over. We'd run things properly, maybe open up several more places, and make a name for ourselves."

"If you had the recipe?" I encouraged.

"Yes, and that's something you'll never get. I'll always have the recipe. Chester thought he had got it right, finally, but he hasn't. People know the difference and I'll never tell." Jeff smiled smugly, a condescending look on his face, but Julia yanked his arm hard and dragged him down until their faces were almost touching.

"Are you insane? All of this to get an ice-cream shop? Just because you didn't get to inherit this place? Blackmail and murder to sell treats to tourists?"

"It's a good earner," said Malc. "Simon made a fortune every year. It's just a shame it was never good enough for him."

"But you aren't telling the truth, are you, Jeff? You're lying," I said, sure of it.

"I'm not. I swear. I admit I played my part, but I didn't kill anyone. It was Chester."

"But why the foot in the sand like that?" asked Trev. "Why did you make it look like someone was buried there?"

"That wasn't me. That was Chester. He thought it was funny. I didn't."

"Funny? Funny! Have you lost your mind?" shrieked Julia. Her skin flushed again, even under the heavy false tan, as she clutched her chest. "Ugh."

"Julia!" Malc screamed as she keeled over sideways and slammed into the filthy yard.

Jeff glanced down, then at us, face a mask of indecision, but the moment Malc bent to help Julia he tore across the yard, jumped into the Land Rover, and was heading towards the farm gate before we had the chance to stop him.

The bulk of the Land Rover tore the gate from the loose posts and Jeff sped over it, kicking up dirt as he skidded down the track then out of sight.

"Go and get him," shouted Malc. "I'll call this in. Hopefully, I can get someone to stop him before he gets to the main road."

We nodded, then raced to the campervan. I whistled for Anxious, who dashed from the workshop with something in his mouth then jumped into the back of the camper as Trev got in the front. I shut the back door, ran around to the driver's side, and we gave chase, clattering over the fallen gate as we sped after Jeff.

Chapter 18

A 1967 T1 is many things. Fun, quirky, cool, and iconic to name a few. What it is not is fast. Or so I thought. Going uphill might be a struggle, but we had absolutely no problem at all hurtling downhill from the farm. If you ignored the uncomfortable ride and the squealing metal as we bounced over bumps, crunched into potholes, or scraped along hedges.

Anxious whined from the rear where he'd wedged himself into a corner, but when we levelled out I called him and he bounded into the front and onto Trev's lap who held him tight, much to my relief.

"I can't believe we're chasing after a killer," Trev gasped, face flushed.

"Neither can I. What is with everyone and ice-cream around here? It's an obsession."

"Simon's was the best," grinned Trev.

"Do you believe Chester killed the guy to put him out of business?"

"It's not that at all."

"No?" I asked, eyebrow raised.

"No, it's because they hated each other. Chester's always been after him, and this was just his excuse. He wanted the recipe and he wanted the business. He really wanted the milk."

"Maybe. Maybe not."

"I get that things became heated and out of hand, but I just can't understand why Jeff would get involved with Chester."

"I'm not so sure he did. At least not how he's telling it. He was desperate," I explained. "He realised everything he'd worked for at the farm was for nothing, so he got together with an accomplice to blackmail Simon into giving up his business and handing it over to them. I assume Jeff would have got a proper legal contract drawn up once Simon agreed, and then he could take over and even use the secret recipe. Whatever the details, it blew up in Jeff's face once his partner attacked Simon."

"You keep saying partner. You mean Chester?" asked Trev.

"We'll get to that in a moment. Jeff gave up Chester too easily. I think he's lying. I think he's smarter than he acts."

"And we didn't even get to the part about what happened to old Brian. Reckon Jeff killed him really?"

"I don't think so. Most likely, Jeff was telling the truth about that, and he just used Brian's death as a way to take the heat off. It certainly worked setting up H."

"Makes sense. Hey, look out!"

An ambulance came tearing up the road and I swerved into the hedge enough to let it pass. I hoped that Julia was okay.

"Where's Jeff going? Where does he think he can get to?"

"He'll be going after Chester. You can count on it."

"How do you know?" I asked my young helper.

"Just a hunch."

"I think you're right. He probably wants to deal with him before the police intercept. It wasn't Chester that killed Simon, and Jeff wants to ensure he never tells."

I floored the accelerator once we were on the main road, but we would never catch up with Jeff no matter how hard I willed Vee to go faster.

"Come on, Vee, you can do it."

Trev and I rocked back and forth in our seats as though it could force her into top speed, but at least we could see Jeff's Land Rover now and were closing as the traffic increased. Suddenly, Jeff slowed, bounced up on the curb, squealed to a halt outside Lovely Stuff, and was out of the vehicle in a flash.

We arrived a moment later and chased after him as the shop door slammed shut and all hell broke loose inside. Not thinking of the consequences, Trev chased in after Jeff as I called for him to wait, so with little choice I ran after him with Anxious at my side, his prize still in his mouth.

"What have you got there?" I asked, but he just looked at me with his head cocked and dashed in through the door as I opened it.

"Say anything else and I swear you'll be next, understand?" Jeff had Chester by the throat and was shaking him like a rag doll. He released the simpering man and shoved him back against the counter where Chester had been cleaning out the display after a presumably lucrative day.

"What have you done?" gasped Chester, rubbing at his throat. "You told, didn't you?"

"Of course I did. They already knew thanks to these idiots." Jeff whirled on Trev and me and growled, "You've got a lot to answer for."

"Us? What did we do? We were just trying to get H free and discover who really killed Simon."

"You snitch," hissed Chester, glaring at Jeff.

"Max figured everything out. He figured you and Simon had come up and one of us had murdered him. Well, I'm not going to prison for murder!"

Chester backed up further, eyes wide in astonishment, and raged, "I'm not taking the blame for that! No way are you pinning this on me. I'm going to come clean. This has gone way too far. You're a liar and a cheat and I will not take the fall for something you both did."

"Both?" asked Trev, glancing to me.

I nodded, then raising my voice so the person in the back room could hear, I called out, "You can stop hiding now. It's over. I know you're in there, Heidi. The game's up."

The room was utterly silent for a moment, and the sigh of Heidi, Chester's employee, was clearly audible. She stomped into the open doorway that led to the store room and glared at everyone as she folded her thin arms across her ice-cream and oil-splattered white apron.

"What's this all about?" she asked, as if daring anyone to accuse her of anything.

"You and your hot head is what got us into this mess," snarled Chester. "We could have just had a profitable business each and Simon would have been out of the picture."

"Kill them all," hissed Heidi, locking eyes on Jeff.

It was as though all the energy drained from Jeff in a single ragged exhale. His shoulders slumped, his head hung, and his entire body just seemed to deflate.

"What the hell is going on?" gulped Trev as he grabbed my arm and took a step back.

"Kill them," shrieked Heidi, advancing on Jeff and getting right up in his face. Jeff kept his head lowered, so Heidi spun to Chester and ordered, "You do it then. Kill those two idiots, and kill Jeff too."

Jeff's head snapped up, and with tears in his eyes, he asked, "You'd see me dead? After everything I did for you? After what we both did?"

"What did you do?" I asked, knowing the answer.

"You're crazy," sighed Chester as he took a step away until we all faced Heidi who was red with rage and wild-eyed.

"You're both insane," shouted Jeff, arms waving wildly. "I can't stand this! I can't live this way. It was her!" Jeff pointed a stubby finger at Heidi; she recoiled at the accusation. "Simon was right where we wanted him, but then Heidi ruined it by taunting him, making fun of him when he was beaten. He changed his mind, refused to make the deal, and laughed in my face. Heidi lost the plot and grabbed an old machete from the workbench and swung at him. He was still laughing right up until he slipped and Heidi pounced on him."

"She killed Simon," gasped Trev.

"Just shut up! Shut up!" wailed Heidi. "He deserved it. Jeff, we could have had his business and the secret recipe, but he lied to us. He said we were pathetic. I got angry."

"Angry? You killed a man and got me to clean up your mess. I should have gone straight to the police, but I loved you. You're out of your mind."

"They're a couple?" whispered Trev, turning to me.

"Yes, but I'm guessing you kept it secret as you knew Chester would fire you if he found out?" I asked Heidi. "He hated Brian so wouldn't let you work here if you were seeing his employee, right?"

"Chester's a petty, sad man," grunted Heidi. She turned to him and admitted, "Jeff and I have been together for years. Biding our time. I knew one day Simon would get into trouble and need bailing out. When we saw the opportunity, we took it. I took it. I convinced Jeff to blackmail Simon so we could get his business and the secret recipe."

"And you promised I could have it if I went along with things once you admitted what you'd done," growled Chester.

"Don't be such an idiot!" laughed Heidi. "We needed your help, I needed an alibi, but we were never going to let you have the recipe. Tell him, Jeff."

"It's true. After Simon died, we knew suspicion would fall on you, so what better way to ensure none of us got into trouble than to have Heidi say you were both at the factory the morning Simon was killed? But no, we were never going to give you the recipe. Not after what you did at the beach. It was sick."

"That was you?" I asked Chester. "All of you were at the beach?"

"No, just me and Chester," admitted Jeff. "I was in a panic after Simon died, so Heidi and I went to Chester's factory and told him what had happened. We knew he'd cover for Heidi if it meant he could get the recipe, and he was happy to oblige."

"You promised me! And you gave me the money and jewellery too. But you're both liars and cheats." Chester leaned against the wall, rubbing at his face, looking like he was about to collapse.

"You deserved nothing after what you did on the beach," should Jeff. "You had to play in the damn sand like an idiot."

"It was funny at the time," chuckled Chester, a man who was clearly as unhinged as the others. "It looked like he'd been buried."

"Idiot," hissed Jeff.

"What do you want?" asked Chester, glancing to the back, I assumed wondering if he could succeed in making a break for it.

"I want to know what you did to Brian. Did you kill him?" I asked, just to be sure.

Chester frowned, then smiled sneakily. "What if I did?"

Jeff growled and lunged, but Chester ducked and stepped aside. "I'll destroy you!" roared Jeff.

"I never touched Brain, I swear. I figured that was you," said Chester, snivelling.

"Of course it wasn't. Enough games! I'm done with this. All of it. I'm coming clean. I just wanted to have a business. Heidi, how could you? I loved you."

"Love doesn't pay the bills, and you promised me we'd have a nice house and sell the best ice-cream in Wales. You're the one who lied. I just took charge because you're too weak to do what needed to be done. Pathetic!"

"He'd have given us what we wanted. You know he would have. But then you had to go and spoil it by getting into a stupid argument and ruining everything."

Heidi just shrugged. "I hated that guy. Him and his stupid milk and stupid secret recipe. I never found it and that was all I wanted. You think I cared about you getting your share? No way! I just wanted the money and the recipe. I would have thrown the jewellery away, but then you had to go and take everything and set up H."

"What was that?" asked Malc as he stepped through the door. "Jeff, you set up H? You took the stolen goods and planted them with the weapon?"

"He did," crowed Chester. "Jeff and Heidi gave me the money and the jewellery to keep quiet about her killing Simon."

"She's the murderer? What have I missed here?" Malc cast a perplexed look my way, but now wasn't the time for a full explanation.

Chester was oblivious to everyone else and said, "Jeff took everything from my place and he already had the machete because Heidi dropped it at the workshop. He set up H. He used the latch from the gate to fool everyone. I assumed Jeff killed Brian." Chester beamed, pleased with himself for his admission, but it didn't seem like anything to be happy about to me as he was admitting just how much he was involved.

"Why H?" I asked.

"Because we needed to get rid of the lot and someone had to take the fall," said Jeff. "I knew Chester here would squeal if he got caught, and he refused to ditch the gear, so I stole it from him and planted everything on H. It was just an utter mess. I got nothing. No business, no future, just nothing."

"Is Julia okay?" I asked Malc.

"Suspected heart attack," he said, face blank. "They took her in the ambulance, then I chased after you. Not that her godson even cares."

"I care," spat Jeff. "But I had to get away. I had to know if Chester would talk."

"Well, I didn't, so there! And I didn't even get the recipe," lamented Chester.

"So you both concocted alibis for each other?" Malc asked Chester and Heidi.

"What if we did? She needed money, and I agreed as long as they gave me what I wanted. I had them over a barrel," laughed Chester.

"That's low," said Trev, pouting.

"And it was all for nothing. No recipe!" wailed Chester.

"That's all you care about? A recipe?" asked Malc, tutting in disgust, a rather animated expression for him.

"They dragged me into their mess and promised me. I hated Simon so didn't care about what they'd done, but no way would I cover for this traitor," he glared at Heidi, "unless I got something good out of it."

"You're all totally nuts," said Trev.

Chapter 19

"I think I might know where the recipe was hidden. In the workshop where you keep your lunchbox, right?" I asked Jeff, unable to hold back my smile.

"How do you know?"

"You found the recipe and you never told?" squealed Chester. "That's all I wanted and you kept it from me?"

"What about me?" snapped Heidi. Her features softened, a sly smile spreading across her flushed face as she asked Jeff, "Honey, did you find the recipe?"

"You didn't deserve it after what you did. What you made me do. I was going to set up on my own. Convince Brian to sell me the milk. How'd you like that?" sneered Jeff.

"Traitor!" Heidi was incandescent with rage, but it was clear she was defeated, unable to put up a fight any longer.

Chester whirled to me and asked, "Where's the recipe?" almost pleading.

I glanced down at Anxious who was sitting rather impatiently, waiting for everyone to realise what he held in his mouth.

"Thank you for this, Anxious," I said, then bent and rubbed his back as I took a rather soggy envelope gently from his mouth.

"That's it? Let me see," pleaded Chester.

Malc stepped forward and warned, "Nobody move another step. Stay right there."

Sirens blared from outside, lights strobed, and police gathered. Malc lifted a hand to tell them to wait and turned back to us.

"Did you read it?" Chester asked Jeff.

"Not yet."

"That's evidence," said Malc. "But the slobber will have ruined any prints."

All eyes were on me as I opened the envelope, lifted out the piece of paper, then handed the envelope to Malc.

"I wonder what the secret ingredient is?" I mused, chef's curiosity taking over. "You did a good thing, Anxious. Well done."

Anxious wagged happily from beside me.

"He deserves a walk after this," said Trev.

"No, don't say it!" I warned, but it was too late.

Anxious spun in a manic circle, frenzy building, then jumped up at me as I lowered my hand to calm him. His claws raked the paper and it tore into two pieces then drifted to the sticky, chequered lino in the sweet-smelling ice-cream shop.

Everyone gasped, but I said, "It's okay. It's ripped, but easy enough to fix."

I bent to retrieve the two halves, but Anxious was still beyond excited, and as the paper stuck fast in a pool of chocolate ice-cream the hungry pooch spied the creamy goodness and snuffled up the lot in a nanosecond, paper included.

Nobody moved. Nobody spoke. Nobody breathed.

Anxious sat, tail wagging, and looked up at me with hope in his eyes.

"Yes, you are a good boy. Would you like your walk now?" I nodded to Malc, said, "We'll be on the beach," then left with Trev beside me and Anxious already out of the door.

Just before the door closed, I heard Chester wail and turned to see him sink to his knees. All he ever wanted in life had been taken from him by a hungry dog keen for a nice walk.

"They all got what they deserved," noted Trev as he flexed his muscles at a pretty young female officer who giggled before receiving a frown from the others who entered the shop at Malc's signal.

"They sure did," I agreed.

Anxious barked with excitement as he spied the sea, so once we were on the beach I unclipped his lead and he tore across the sand, joyous and carefree as always.

"So the secret dies with Anxious?" said Trev. "That's kinda sad. Simon might not have been the nicest guy, but he sure made the best ice-cream."

"Unless someone happened to get a look at the recipe before it was eaten," I said with a wink.

"You didn't, did you?" gasped Trev.

I zipped my mouth shut and threw away the key.

Some secrets shall never be told.

We were on the return leg of our quick walk when I spied DI Malc Anderson plodding along the beach, the fact he was so nondescript making him stand out against the few remaining tanned bodies soaking up the last of the sun's goodness.

When we met, he stopped and sighed rather dramatically.

"Hey," I said.

"Hey," he replied.

"Guess I should say one too," grinned Trev. "Hey."

There was an awkward, extended silence, then Malc broke it and admitted, "You did a fantastic job. I had my suspicions about Jeff, but it was hard to broach the subject with Julia. She thought the world of that man. He's let her down so badly."

"I understand."

"What really tipped you off that he was involved? Just a hunch, or that you saw him today coming out of the bank? That's no reason to suspect him."

"No, not that."

"Of course! You spoke to Brian's daughter and she told you about the will. But that doesn't explain how you figured out who killed Simon."

"It was something Trev said about him cleaning the beach several times a week with the machinery. It got me to thinking. Understand?"

"Not really," said Malc.

"Okay, you got me. We spoke to Rosa, Brian's daughter, and she told us about Jeff being very angry that he wasn't inheriting the farm like he'd been promised. That could tip you over the edge if you thought for years it would be yours. But he never said he wasn't going to inherit it to Julia?"

"Not as far as I know."

"Right, so when things went wrong with Simon and he found Brian dead, Jeff figured he might as well use the old farmer's death and get himself out of any trouble or suspicion by pretending Brian was murdered and it was Simon's killer who did it. But it didn't work out like that."

"No, it didn't. Far from it."

"But it was the clean beach that finally let me put everything together. Jeff was here, and nobody thought about it. He had the machinery to clean the beach, which meant he could easily drop the body down by the water. Didn't you think to ask him?"

"I didn't even know that was a thing," admitted Malc. "And even if I had known, I wouldn't have assumed it was Jeff. There was no link between him and Simon."

"Apart from ice-cream and thus Chester and Heidi. I'm sure they're all keen to talk now. It had been bugging me how readily Heidi offered up an alibi for Chester, when the truth was she was ensuring she was the one with an alibi. Sure, Chester went along with things and is clearly deranged as he buried Simon's foot, but most of this was Heidi manipulating and taking advantage of the greed of the others. It's all very sad."

"I'm sure I'll get the full story from them all. They're already falling over each other to talk. Seems like Jeff loved Heidi and would do anything for her, but maybe she pushed him too far? Again, you did good. Thanks." Malc turned to Trev and said, "You too. Thank you."

"Our pleasure. Think we'll get a medal or something? Maybe a mention in the paper?"

"We don't get medals for solving crimes. That's our job."

"Did you just smile?" I laughed. "You did, didn't you?"

"I don't smile." Malc glared at us, then his face softened and the corners of his mouth twitched. "Maybe I smile sometimes."

"So, that's it? Think it will be easy to convict them?"

"Yes, very. We all heard what was said, and you will both have to make statements, but there's no chance of them getting away with this. Both men already admitted Heidi killed Simon and they helped cover it up. A team's on its way to the workshop, and as you said, there will be fingerprints, blood, and all kinds of evidence to link Heidi to Simon's murder now we know who it was. It's a done deal."

"I can't believe I helped solve a murder," said Trev, beaming with pride.

"You did very well. Maybe you should consider joining the force," suggested Malc.

"What, and cover up this? No chance." Trev flexed his biceps and jiggled his pecs, grinning. "I like the beach too much, and I save lives in a different way, but it's all important."

"It is," agreed Malc. "I'm going to the hospital to check on Julia and to fill her in on what happened. Hopefully, she's doing okay."

"Give her our best, and will it be alright if I visit her tomorrow?"

"I'm sure it will."

Malc plodded slowly back up the beach to the road, looking like he had the weight of the world on his shoulders.

"He doesn't seem very happy that this is over with," noted Trev.

"He's worried about his partner. That will be his main concern now."

"I hope she'll be alright. That must have been scary for her. Sad too. I wonder how close her and Jeff were?"

"Pretty close by the seems of it. But she must have known there was something not quite right about him. People don't just suddenly turn to extortion, covering up a murder, and planting evidence without there being some sort of sign, surely?"

"Mate, I wouldn't know. I've never met a murderer before."

"Unfortunately, I have. Come on, let's go and break the news to Min and Rosa. They'll be relieved they aren't in any danger."

It was a short walk back to the pub, and we found the ladies inside, talking rather loudly and both clearly on their second or third glass of wine.

We explained what had happened and both were beyond relieved, but Rosa was clearly exhausted by the whole ordeal as not only had she lost her father, but he'd been used to dupe the police and point the finger at an innocent man.

"Are you sure Dad just died of natural causes?"

"That's what they all said. Chester assumed Jeff killed him, but Jeff admitted to just using his death to take the heat off. I'm guessing he knew Chester had a screw loose and didn't want him blabbing. As for Heidi, I don't know what to think. She played them off against one another, and they let her because they were greedy. Framing H was the perfect opportunity to divert everyone's attention. Sorry, it's a lot to take in."

"You poor thing. It's so awful," said Min.

"It is, but at least Dad really did go out how he always said he wanted to. He was with his girls, and he loved those cows so much."

We walked with Rosa back to the road and she decided to stay the night in a hotel. We stood with her until we were sure they had a room, then said our goodbyes.

Walking back to the campsite, Trev cleared his throat, then blurted, "Are we still having dinner? I'm starving."

"I'd forgotten all about it, and it's getting late. But I can do something, yes. In fact, I have the perfect recipe in mind."

"As long as it's not a recipe for murder," laughed Min.

"So lame," said Trev, shaking his head.

"What? That was a killer line," Min pouted. Her eyes brightened, and she asked, "You liked that one, right? It was a killer line?"

"Min, both jokes are awful," I chided. "Beyond cliched."

"Well, I thought it was funny. So, what's for dinner?"

"You're staying?"

"I'll leave early tomorrow, but I promise I won't rush off without saying goodbye. If that's okay?"

"Of course. It will be great."

Happy to have a distraction, I spent the next hour showing Trev how to prepare a glorious but speedy one-pot meatballs and spaghetti dish. He was both amazed and dumbfounded that you could make such incredible food in a single pot in such a reasonable amount of time, and ate more than anyone, not that I minded.

After speaking to Malc about giving a statement in the morning and checking that Julia would make it—she was recovering well—Trev left to spread the word about our escapade. Min and I settled down to a very quiet, somewhat subdued evening, just the two of us.

Early the next morning, I hurried for my morning pee, then returned to find her ready and the coffee made.

"I told you I wouldn't leave without saying goodbye."

"You did. Promise me something else?"

"Sure, anything." She smiled, her eyes twinkling with amusement and happiness.

"That you'll come back soon? Wherever I am."

"You can count on it. You can't get rid of me that easily."

"Good, and one other thing?"

"Yes?"

"Never get me to make ice-cream," I laughed. "Even if I do know the secret recipe."

Min groaned, Anxious barked, and I sat and drank my coffee.

Chapter 20

"Put a T-shirt on," I hissed, glancing around and noting the bemused, but mostly lascivious, glances from the nurses. The orderlies, doctors, and even the security guard wore the same expressions. Envy, admiration, plus a healthy dose of confusion.

"Don't try to change me, Max," said Trev happily as we marched along the corridor towards the ward where DI Julia Bennet was in recovery. He flexed his pecs and smiled happily at everyone we passed, getting coquettish giggles and girlish laughter from a group of nurses huddled by a counter.

"Wouldn't dream of it. Come on, we can't stay too long, as Anxious wasn't happy about being left outside."

"This is it here."

We paused at the entrance to a small ward of a half-dozen beds, searching for Julia. She was at the far end on the left, sitting up and looking so different it took me a moment to recognise her. "There she is."

"Is that her? Are you sure?"

"Yes. Come on."

We passed the small groups of people there for visiting hours, and I tried to breathe normally, the strong antiseptic smell catching in my throat, the ever-present disinfectant tang putting me in a perpetual state of a sneeze wanting to burst free but never quite making it. Harsh overhead lights lit up the room in a most unappealing way, highlighting dark shadows under Julia's eyes as we got closer.

"How are you doing?" I asked softly.

"Fine," boomed Julia happily. "Best few days of rest I've had in years. I should have a minor heart attack more often." People turned at the loud voice, but Julia didn't care; she was confident and secure in her own skin, same as always.

"You look so different," said Trev, shuffling about.

"Give her the gift," I encouraged, smiling at Julia.

"No chocolates?" she grumbled, shaking her head.

"Sorry, but we figured fresh fruit might be better considering you had a heart attack."

"That's okay, and thank you."

Trev placed the basket of fruit on the small table then stepped back, clearly concerned Julia's condition might be contagious. He stood beside me, arms crossed, looking everywhere but at the patient.

"Don't like hospitals, eh?" she asked.

"Not really. They freak me out. It smells weird and everyone's sick."

"Same. It's why I never get ill," I agreed.

"Make that three of us. I can't wait to get out of here, but I'm also having the time of my life. It's so relaxing, and I get to catch up on a load of TV. I've got my tablet, so I've been binge-watching."

"How long are you in for?" I asked.

"A few more days. It's already been three, and honestly I'm getting beyond bored. Bored is nice, but I'm missing out on the action. And I don't feel like myself without the fake tan and the make-up. Don't even get me started on having to wear this monstrosity of a gown, or whatever they call it. Who the hell invented such a ridiculous thing?" Julia tugged at the requisite gown all the patients wore; another reason why she looked so utterly different.

"You do look kinda pale," said Trev with a smile.

"Do you think that's helping?" I hissed.

"Dunno. Is it?"

"Not really, no," said Julia with a wan smile. "But thank you for coming. I am assuming you both have an ulterior motive?"

"You know us too well," I laughed. "We did want to see how you were doing, and to say sorry for causing you to get so ill."

"It wasn't your fault. It was my terrible godson's."

"Yes, but we sprung it on you, and then you had a heart attack. We feel responsible," I said.

"Don't. It was him, not you. Max, you did a great job figuring it out. Trev, you too. Although there's less chance of me having a second heart attack if you put some clothes on. It's making me wish I was a few decades younger."

"In your dreams," grinned Trev.

"Oh, the things I could teach you," sighed Julia, a faraway look in her eyes.

I cleared my throat and said, "So, what's the news? What happened? I tried Malc, but you know how he is. Not exactly a chatterbox."

"No, he isn't. But he's a good guy and has visited every day. I think he might have smiled once."

"We saw that too!" gushed Trev. "At least, I think we did."

"They let H go," I said. "He's quite the star at the campsite. He'll be getting free beers for weeks. Everyone wants to hear about his stay in jail and what it was like. He's loving the attention."

"I bet. That was an unfortunate incident, but when you get evidence that strong, you have to follow up on it."

"We understand, and so does he. He doesn't have any hard feelings. He's a chilled guy."

"Seemed it, if extremely flaky. It was clear the whole thing was a set-up from the start, and very obvious, which is why we were going all-out to solve it. But you beat us to it, Max. Again." Julia looked deep into my eyes, saying more with a look than with words. She didn't hold a grudge, but was rather annoyed with herself at the same time.

"It was just one of those things," I shrugged. "We bumped into Rosa and she told us about Jeff being angry at not inheriting the farm. But it was Trev mentioning that Jeff cleaned the beach that made me sure."

"And we should have thought of that. I never knew he did it, but the fact the beach was cleaned didn't even cross my mind. That's sloppy police work. We were looking for a motive involving gangsters because of Simon's history, when we should have been following up on a feud over ice-cream instead." Julia shook her head and laughed, hearty and deep, then winced as she rubbed her chest.

"Word is, Lucy's off the hook with the gangsters," said Trev. "They know about the money and jewellery being found and told Lucy she's in the clear, no debt owed."

"How come?" asked Julia.

"Guess they don't want to risk any of it coming back on them. And Lucy's gone over the books and there's more money than she thought. The factory is already being fixed while she waits for the insurance to come through, so everyone keeps their jobs and the business will be open within days."

"That's so good to hear. I'm glad there's a happy ending to this." Julia thumped her chest as she wheezed.

"You okay? Do you need the nurse?"

"No, I'm good. Just somewhat freaked out, I guess. I'm going to lose the weight when I get out of here, and start taking some exercise. I need to chill out too. That's the number one killer. Stress."

"You need to do what we do and get yourself a campervan. No mortgage, no bills. Freedom," said Trev.

"And they cost a fortune! I haven't got that kind of money. No, I like my house, my life, my husband, and my friends. I'm content where I am, but I need to deal with the stress of the job better. But listen to me rambling on. You don't need to hear about that. So, what's next for you, Max? You sticking around?"

"By the look on your face, I'm guessing you hope I say the answer is no," I laughed.

"What, and miss out on you solving all the crimes? Whatever gave you that idea?" Julia winked, warm and friendly, but she also spoke the truth.

"I'm leaving tomorrow. Anxious and I are keen to explore, and Min has agreed to meet me in Portmeirion in a few days."

"Hey, I've heard about that place," said Trev.

"I've been there. It's amazing. It's like a miniature village with all kinds of incredible architecture brought in from around the world by a collector. Can't think of his name, but you'll love it. There's a large raised pond in the middle of it, lots of walks in the woods, and a small beach too. Just a tiny thing when the tide is out. The trees are from every corner of the earth, with some amazing huge redwoods. You guys getting back together?"

"I wish. But no. Min said she's free on the weekend, which will give me time to recover and get settled, then we'll meet at Portmeirion just for a few hours."

"You want her back, eh?"

"I do. We'll see what happens, but I don't know what the future will hold."

"That's the beauty of life, Max. The anticipation is what keeps us going day after day. You simply never know what's around the corner and that's the exciting part. It's why I love being a detective. Sometimes more than others." Julia tutted, clearly still rankled about not solving the crime.

"Don't worry, I'll be off your patch tomorrow, so no more interfering from me."

"Good. Okay, time for you both to go. I'm tired, and I want to finish my shows before they boot me out of here. I've got years to catch up on in a few days."

"Get well soon," I said.

"See you around," said Trev with a nod, then wandered over to the entrance and waited for me.

"He's a good lad," noted Julia.

"He is. I've quite enjoyed hanging out with him. I wish he'd put a damn T-shirt on though."

"I don't," giggled Julia, glancing over at him already deep in conversation with several nurses.

"See you soon," I said, nodding.

"Not if I see you first." Julia smiled, then reached over and picked up her tablet. "Oh, one more thing," she called out.

I hurried back over and asked, "Yes?"

"How'd you know Jeff and Heidi had a thing going on? That's what this all boiled down to, right? You knew they were a couple."

"Trev said something at the pub about the possibility that Jeff was the culprit because he wanted money to buy a house to start a family. Then a detail I'd forgotten about clicked. When I bought an ice-cream and Heidi was keen to offer up the alibi for herself and Chester, I noticed a smudge on her apron."

"She worked in an ice-cream shop. They're always covered in the stuff."

"This was more like an oil stain. It just spread when she rubbed it. Jeff's always got oil-stained hands from being in the workshop. They must have met up earlier that day and he got her apron greasy."

"Damn," whistled Julia. "You really do pick up on the details."

"Told you," I said with a wink, then waved as I left.

After collecting Trev from his adoring fans, we left the hospital, retrieved Anxious who was asleep but very pleased to see me, then headed back to the campsite.

"What's got into you?" I asked Trev as I took the turn into Sanctuary.

"Look," he grinned.

I pulled to a stop at H's bus, unable to go anywhere because the top of the campsite was blocked by people and vehicles.

"What's going on?"

"You'll see. Park here, and let me show you."

Confused, I got out and followed Anxious and Trev towards the mass of people and vehicles forming a ring around H's van. Trev beckoned me on and as we got to the bus everyone started clapping. H was beaming from where he stood outside his home with the others, their eyes locked on me. I felt uncomfortable and self-conscious, but happy too. Warmed by the goodwill emanating from my fellow travellers.

"We made you a banner," declared H as he indicated the large sign draped across the bus.

"Thank you for the Max Effort," I read, chuckling. "But I don't understand. What's this for?"

"For saving me. For saving the town from the bad guys, and for being so cool about it. We all appreciate it, right?" he shouted.

People cheered and surged forward to congratulate me on solving the case. I made sure that Trev joined me and Anxious, and both received either belly rubs or pats on the back, although it got rather confusing and I wasn't sure which was meant for which or who enjoyed the adoration more.

"You didn't have to do this," I told H. "But thank you."

"Dude, you saved my life. I couldn't handle it being locked up, and I was freaked out, man. With the murder weapon, the jewellery, and everything else on the bus, I thought I was going down for life. I'll never forget this, Max. Never. You're welcome back here any time, and I hope you do come back. Maybe same time next year?"

"I think I might take you up on that offer," I said, wondering what it would be like to spend a whole year travelling around the country then returning to see familiar faces. Friends. More friends. I was part of a community and the feeling was growing every day. That this life we had chosen really was something special, and I didn't want to change it for anything.

When Anxious and I finally retreated to the campervan in the early hours of the morning, it was with a groan when I opened up Vee. "I forgot to unfold the bed again, Anxious." Nevertheless, I was whistling as I sorted out my sleeping arrangements, and already looking forward to the next leg of our trip.

Anxious sat and watched me, yawning, then jumped onto the bed the moment it was made.

As we settled for a much-needed sleep, I stroked Anxious' back and confided, "Hopefully, we can find time to relax properly. So far, vanlife is exhausting. We'll go to a nice place in the country where the weather will be a little cooler than on the coast, and just take it easy. There's a list of pubs in that book I bought where you can park there for free for a few nights, so we'll do that. Just a calm, quiet place with a river, maybe do some fishing, and just soak up the country air." I kept quiet about meeting up with Min, as the last thing he needed right now was to get excited.

Anxious licked my hand, then sighed as he rolled onto his back and his legs flopped open. I fell asleep rubbing his belly, and didn't wake until the morning was almost over.

It was time to go.

The End

But it isn't really! Read on for a stunning one-pot recipe and an update about what to expect next for Max and Anxious as their vanlife adventure continues.

Recipe

Meatballs and Spaghetti

Everyone and their momma has a meatball recipe they insist is the absolute best and dare you to argue. You can get picky with your tomatoes, argue over seasoning, come to blows over what meat to use, and even draw swords over the pasta. One thing I can guarantee is that if you use good ingredients you're happy with then this is a foolproof recipe. It doesn't take an inordinate amount of time either.

The joy of one-pot cooking is that you are taking some of the stress out of your culinary endeavours. If you are working in a confined space, or simply want to streamline the cooking process, it should still be fun. Cooking should be enjoyable, not a chore, and going back-to-basics is one way to look at it in a new, more forgiving light.

So my advice is to choose the best ingredients you can, but not be unduly concerned about the exact brand of tomatoes or pasta, and just go with the flow and enjoy the end result. As with all Mediterranean cooking, good bread to hand is always worth the investment, and decent olive oil should always be part of everyone's basic stores, even those on the road.

Let's begin.

Ingredients

- Minced meat around 500g / 1lb. I use half pork and half beef
- One egg
- Fresh breadcrumbs - 2 tbsp
- Dried thyme - 2 tsp

- Garlic - 3 cloves crushed
- Olive oil - 2-3 tbsp
- A small onion - finely diced
- One carrot - finely diced
- One celery stick - finely diced
- Rosemary - finely chopped - 1 tsp
- Passata - 1 carton
- Balsamic vinegar - 1 tbsp
- Chicken stock cube
- Tomato puree - 2 tbsp
- Spaghetti - 250g / 8oz
- Just boiled water - 600ml / 1pt
- Salt & black pepper
- Grated Parmesan to serve

Method

Of course you can mix up the herbs, stock, and even veggies. A little chopped sage in the meatballs would be great. Peppers would work well. Olives are a fine addition. Use the ground meat of your choice. Turkey if you're that way inclined, but a mixture of beef and pork offers, for me, the best mixture of both flavour and texture. For a really simple version you could replace the whole meatball mix with high quality butcher's sausages (just split the casing and form balls with the sausage meat). We enjoy this with spaghetti though it is easier to serve using almost any other pasta shape. Fresh breadcrumbs soaked in milk would be ideal but perhaps a step too far for campervan cooking.

This, then, is how I usually make this when I'm not bothered about a few extra bowls to wash, but don't want the oven on or extra pans to contend with.

- Mix the meat, egg, breadcrumbs, thyme and one clove of garlic, a little salt and pepper in a bowl. Using wet hands form the mixture into walnut sized balls.
- Heat the oil in a wide casserole and fry the meatballs over a medium heat. You want them golden but they don't need to cook through yet. Depending on your casserole size you might find this easier to do in batches.
- Once you have some golden balls and some tasty sticky bits on the bottom of the pan, it's time to add the onions. Pile the meatballs to one side, making room for the onions. Turn the heat down and cook until translucent.
- Add in the carrot, celery, and the rest of the garlic. Stir through and cook for another five minutes or so until everything is shiny and starting to colour gently.
- Tip in the rosemary, passata, balsamic, stock cube, and tomato puree. Stir everything well, bring to the boil, then turn down to a gentle simmer and leave to cook for ten minutes.
- Now add the pasta, water, and season to taste. Simmer for ten to twelve minutes depending on your chosen pasta.
- This can be a faff to serve if you're using spaghetti! Use tongs to fish the pasta out and arrange in bowls or plates, then top with the meatballs and sauce.
- Serve sprinkled with Parmesan alongside some awesome artisan sourdough and a green salad. *Gustoso!*

From the Author

Max sure seems to get caught up in a lot of adventures! Maybe next time things will be different and we can just read about him sitting for a few days and reading a good book while Anxious snores on the bed.

As if!

Get ready for more one-pot wonders, guest appearances from folks who have already become firm fan favourites, and a hefty dose of murder, mystery, and mayhem on the open road. Hopefully with a nice pint to wash it all down.

Continue Max's Campervan Case Files in Poisoned at the Pub. It'a a real pickle of a problem. And yes, that is a clue!

Be sure to stay updated about new releases and fan sales. You'll hear about them first. No spam, just book updates at www.authortylerrhodes.com

You can also follow me on Amazon and connect with me on Facebook:

- www.amazon.com/stores/author/B0BN6T2VQ
- www.facebook.com/authortylerrhodes/

Printed in Great Britain
by Amazon

43342570R00111